Those hot, pouty, warm, wet, red lips capture me in their torturous grasp.

For a split second, I assume one of us made a mistake. But when I attempt to pull away, my lower lip gets caught between hers as she holds them together.

Holy Shit. That's no accident.

"You okay, Angel Eyes?"

She nods but doesn't speak. She struggles to pull it together, but can't quite nail it.

This is a huge night for us, but I've got to make a choice. Sort this out with her now or bury it for good.

"You want to get out here?" Fuck. I can't believe I just said that. I can't believe I meant it.

"God yes." She rasps.

-As

WISH UP ON A ROCK STAR

A Steamy Wrong Sister Romance

ANNABETH SARYU

ANNABETH SARYU
Heal. Heart. Happy Endings

AUTHOR'S NOTE

This manuscript was written by an American author using an American English dictionary and style guide. Grammar, spelling and word usage may vary from your local customs and practices.

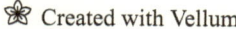 Created with Vellum

To everyone who survived COVID-19.
In loving memory of those who did not.

CHAPTER ONE

ROSE

"*D*on't worry. Everything will be fine," Raelynn calls from the super-sized bathroom where she's applying her makeup.

"Famous last words," I mumble, perched on her massive four-poster bed as we discuss our plans for the evening through the open door.

"Come on, Rosalie. Lighten up. The album release party for *Down the Rabbit Hole* is at the HotZone. It'll be smokin'."

"Rae, that's your scene, not mine," I remind her. Again.

"I'm aware," she sighs. "And I'm sorry. But you really need to do this for me, okay?"

Our eyes meet in the large mirror's reflection. Without

her supermodel veneer of flawless makeup, a few hair-pieces, and a designer outfit, the barriers between us aren't an obstacle.

Yet.

"I already said I'd do it," I complain, breaking eye contact first. "But you know I hate this."

She gets up from her dressing table, exits the bath-room, and comes to sit beside me. With the length of our legs touching, we do what we have since childhood. Raelynn gives me a hug, and I lay against her shoulder.

"I will straighten this out. But right now, I can't." She squeezes me with an edge of trepidation in her voice. "And you know I wouldn't ask if Sergio wasn't important to me."

Sergio is my sister's new boyfriend. I've never seen her this worked up about a guy. It might even be true love.

But there's one problem, and his name is Wes Anders.

Yes, *that* Wes Anders. Rock god to die for, founder and lead vocalist of *Jester's Edge*.

From the moment they made their first red-carpet appearance together, he and Raelynn were an insta-thing. In fact, it gave such a lift to both of their careers they made it official. No, not happily ever after official. Worse.

Contractually obligated at the insistence of their agents official.

Because of the huge attention boost their combined hotness creates, they're set to attend a series of high-profile events together, including tonight's party at the HotZone.

Naturally, the contracts were finalized long before Rae met Sergio. Raelynn hasn't said much, but from what I gather, the enigmatic half-Russian half-Indian billionaire doesn't believe her relationship with Wes is fake.

I don't blame him.

After all, women embellish their single status all the time for a chance with him. Even though my twin is a no bullshit type of gal, Sergio apparently hasn't figured that out yet. But she's not the first model he's dated, and Raelynn and Wes really do generate lots of heat together. Sergio's wrong about her, but I understand why.

How does Raelynn meet her contractual obligations while staying in the good graces of her hot new man?

Me.

Tonight, I'm standing in for Raelynn. As Raelynn.

That's right. I'm impersonating my super-model sister at a media event for a multi-platinum rock band's latest album.

We've both lost our collective minds.

Now, I *have* done this before. Indie movie premieres, gallery exhibits, even theatre productions. All events my sister wasn't paid to be at but felt would benefit her image to be seen in attendance.

While some of the events were great, I don't like impersonating her, and I've never shown up for a paid gig in her place. Tonight is over the line.

"Um, won't anyone notice that I'm not you?" I argue. "We might be twins, but we're very different."

"It will be packed with people buzzing on the energy, attention, and god knows what else." She shrugs. "You'll be fine."

"What if I pull this is off and someone you know believes I'm you?"

3

"Don't worry about it. Stand there and smile, say nothing, or the least amount possible. Just make sure they get plenty of pics. You should be out in one hour, tops."

I take a gulp of air. "What about Wes?"

Now it's Rae's turn to sigh. "Wes knows the drill, and all eyes will be on him. He'll be surrounded by throngs of people eager to see and be seen with the band. Besides, we haven't actually spoken in over a month. Either we go through our agents, or he texts, and you handle those for me."

Her reminder makes me uneasy.

"Can't you tell Wes about Sergio?" I plead.

"Absolutely not."

"Why?" My frustration surfaces.

"First, I'm contractually required to show up tonight. Telling the truth is more trouble than it's worth," she replies.

"Are you sure about that?"

"Positive." She gives me a firm shake. "My agreement with Wes is strictly professional, and that's how it's going to stay. My private life is none of his business," she insists.

"Fine." I wriggle free from Raelynn's embrace. "But this is it. I can't keep pretending to be you. For starters, I'm ten, maybe fifteen pounds heavier than you, and I refuse to do a wheat-grass diet or any other BS."

Rae's a top model, but size two is a constant struggle for her. She never lets herself get larger than a four, even when she's on a break. That's what it takes to be tops at the lingerie fashion shows. But I can tell she misses beer, pizza, and ice cream.

4

Me? Runs along the beach before work and tennis on the weekends gets me to a fit size six. But since I refuse to give up micro-brews and Candy's Custom Cupcakes, it works out to an eight in the dressing room. Most of the time it works well enough. The right clothes, a few slenderizing undergarments, some flattering camera angles, and no one's any wiser.

"You look good tonight," she interrupts my thoughts. "What are you, a six right now?"

"Stop trying to distract me with flattery." I hate when she does that. There's no hiding it from Raelynn, she can spot an extra or lost pound on me from across the room.

"I am not." She crosses her legs, revealing her fuzzie-licious slipper-sandals, a stark contrast to her elegant robe. "You have your own beauty, plus the luxury of a nice wheatie pitcher of beer whenever. Can't I be envious for once?"

"My brand of beer-loving beauty will get us busted." I stand and pace the length of her bedroom. "I don't care to be standing in front of the blades when all of this hits the fan."

"That won't happen tonight. Trust me." Raelynn leaps off the bed, her designer silk robe rustling as she walks to the center of the room and blocks my path. "Sergio's hosting a private fundraiser at this house for Secret Santas who really wish to remain anonymous. No pictures, no phones, no media. No chance Wes or our agents will find out."

"Well, at least you're covered." I sigh. "What about the launch tonight?"

"Relax. It's a costume party." Raelynn nods and offers me a knowing look. "It will be big, busy, chaotic."

"A costume party?" I gasp. "Rae, I have nothing to wear."

She gives me her mischievous smile, the one that sold millions of tubes of smokey eyeliner number four. "Not to worry. I do."

Raelynn spins around and marches with determination to the garage sized closet attached to her bathroom. I rub my temples, then collapse onto the satin bedspread. The cool fabric soothes the back of my neck and shoulders, instilling a momentary calm.

This sucks.

Impersonating my sister always stresses me out, and I loathe the idea of deceiving Wes Anders any more than I have.

More than Raelynn knows about.

My thoughts are interrupted by the distant snap of a light switch. The rustle of plastic and the click of a door are an inadequate warning for my sister's next surprise.

"Ta da!" Raelynn announces with a flourish.

I prop myself up on both elbows and feel my eyes widen in shock.

"What the hell is that?"

CHAPTER TWO

ROSE

*O*h. My. God.

After Raelynn squeezed me into this, *this* hooker-red bare all-bustier with matching thong, she went to work on my make-up. I never wear it. Well, maybe some eyeliner and lipstick on a great day, but that's it. Tonight, she used all the jars in her arsenal, every trick in the book. And damn it, my supermodel sister knows what the hell she's doing in that department.

The result?

I look like some sex mistress emcee in an erotic para-normal revue.

In keeping with the theme of the album and party, my costume resembles a sexy mad hatter, complete with a large purple velvet top hat and a harlequin face mask. To

7

make matters worse, she embellished my outfit with a pair of shiny, thigh-high, patent leather boots.

Fuck me boots.

At first, I hesitated, but this stupid costume is so skimpy the boots made me feel less exposed. But as I stare down at them now, the gold and red medallion buttons draw attention all on their own.

Damn it. I never should have agreed to this. Nervous as I am about a major wardrobe malfunction, it's seeing Wes Anders that makes me shiver in both fear and anticipation.

Full disclosure. I've been crushing on him for a while.

Besides being Raelynn Tailor's low-key twin sister, I'm also her personal assistant, which means my duties include handling work-related phone calls and texts. Raelynn has multiple phone numbers, one for her private calls plus additional ones for people who need to reach her but whom she doesn't want to deal with directly.

That's my job.

Since Wes Anders fell firmly into the 'business' category, communication with him became part of my daily grind. It started with his texts to my sister, which go straight to my phone.

At first, he'd text her simple questions about dates, times, reminders, contacts. Since they were easy to answer, I never explained that I was her assistant.

I took guilty pleasure in being on the receiving end of his potent charm.

Over the course of a few months, I discovered that Wes unguarded is hilarious,

*WES: Why is masturbation just like procras-
tination?*
ME: (as Rae)?
*WES: It's all good until you realize you're only
screwing yourself.*
ME: Are you procrastinating?
WES: How could you tell?
ME: Because you're texting me…

romantic,

*WES: Do supermodels enjoy being told they're
attractive? Or do they assume it's a shameless
ploy to get in their panties.? Asking for a
friend…*

and even protective.

*WES: They did WHAT? Do I need to kick some-
one's ass?*

I looked forward to his texts and started enjoying my
'work,' and it soon became clear that our exchanges
morphed into something unexpected.

That's when things became problematic.

Raelynn told me that Wes had become super flirtatious
during their scheduled appearances, and he seemed
confused when she rebuffed him. After that, responding to
his texts made me feel a like an impostor. I tried to tone
them down, make them shorter and less engaging, even
delayed answering.

But it was too little too late. When Rae and Sergio got together, she flat out ghosted Wes. I haven't told a soul and confessing at this point would cause a monumental shitstorm.

Hopefully, he'll be too pre-occupied to give a fuck.

As the Mercedes sedan rolls to the curb outside of HotZone, I peer out at the crowd. A bunch of well-dressed club goers form a line near the front door. There must be several hundred people here, not including friends and industry insiders who aren't expected to stand in line.

"Wait here, please," Huey, my sister's regular bodyguard, says from the front passenger seat.

From my car window, I watch as he strides to HotZone's front entrance, speaks to the bouncers, then disappears inside.

Whenever Raelynn attends events with a public audience, her agency hires private security from a top Los Angeles firm. Huebert, or Huey, is her primary personal protection specialist. They're perfect for each other, professionally speaking.

My sister is an A-list celebrity model who doesn't deal with imminent threats but runs into occasional problems. People try to touch her. A lot. It's highly intrusive at best, while the worst cases are fricking scary. At three hundred plus pounds, Huey is the ultimate gentle giant. He's got a boyish face, a soft voice, and a death glare that would turn a ghost pale. Crowds take one look at him and keep their hands to themselves.

A moment later, he exits HotZone and approaches the car.

"We're good," Huey tells the driver. "Right up here.

Park on the side of the building. We'll take her in the front."

"Both of you?" I ask.

"Yes, ma'am. They'll want some pics of you entering the party by yourself. I'll focus on getting you inside while Doug watches the crowd. Easy-peasy," he says.

Doug. I make a mental note. We've never met, so I'm not sure if he's ever worked for Raelynn before. They always send Huey, but I don't know about the second man because he remains in the car.

"Thank you both."

Doug looks at me for a moment in the rearview mirror, then glances at Huey, who shrugs and nods at him to drive. When the car's parked, we're about a hundred feet from the main entryway. Doug goes around the back of the large sedan and waits. Huey gets out, checks the area, and then opens my door.

"Ready, Ms. Tailor?"

I take a deep, steady breath. "Yes."

"Walk between us," he instructs me in a low voice.

I nod and do what he says. My six-inch stiletto heels leave me nervously eyeing sidewalk cracks. When I approach the line outside Club HotZone, the crowd reacts.

"Raelynn Tailor! Hey!"

"Hi! Hi! Hi, Raelynn!"

"Raelynn, look this way, please!"

This often happens when Raelynn makes an appearance. But I'm usually the quiet assistant in the background. This time, I'm the center of attention, and that's never worked for me.

The noise, crush, and rush of people make me hyperaware that my costume doesn't cover my ass and that I can barely walk in six-inch heels, let alone gallop gracefully across uneven pavement looking happy and glamourous. What worries me the most is that twin or not, I'm no Raelynn Tailor, and someone's going to figure it out.

Before awkward panic makes me do something stupid, Huey put his catcher's mitt-sized hand underneath my armpit. With no visible effort, he lifts me slightly off the ground and I'm suddenly gliding past the line with old-school Rita Hayworth speed and style. He doesn't release his grip until we're inside with the door shut behind us.

I blow out a relieved breath, and beside me, he does the same.

"Ready to tell me what's going on?" Huey hovers over me, speaking in an urgent whisper.

"Wha- what do you mean?"

"Come on, Rosalie."

"What did you say?" Heat rushes down to my gut.

"The name you told me I could call you when you interviewed me about working for your sister. Remember?"

"Oh God," I gasp. "You know?"

"I do." Huey's eyes scan the room as Doug talks to the bouncers. "It's my job to know my clients, how they act, and how people will react to them. Tell me what's going on."

"My sister agreed to be here tonight as part of her PR contract with Wes Anders, but she couldn't make it." My arms fold. "Since all Rae needed to do was show up and look good for an hour, she thought I could... fill in for her,

12

while avoiding apologies or additional demands from Wes and his management group."

"And it didn't occur to either of you to tell your security team?"

"I'm sorry, but you're not my security team. Since the evening started, I've been trying to keep my head down and mouth shut." I feel exposed, compromised, and vulnerable. "This isn't going to work, is it?"

"You look like her, especially with your dark hair concealed," he admits. "But there's more to it than looks. Her job comes with a lot of demands and exposure, and you've got to embrace that to thrive." Huey blows out a breath. "Sister or not, it's one hell of an ask."

"You're right. I've had a front-row seat to my sister's life for a long time, and it's not something that fills me with envy. I have my own career aspirations, but until those happen, this is how things are for now."

"Don't wait too long, Rosalie," he warns me. "Big careers and personalities have a way of consuming the people around them."

"Will you help get through tonight? Please?" I beg.

Huey studies me for a minute, then nods. "You look fucking fabulous in that costume." His eyes meet mine. "Embrace it. Own it. There's not a straight guy in here who wouldn't give his left nut to be with you."

"Huey—"

"Don't act stunned. Be bored, annoyed, distracted. I'm not the only person who's going to say things like that to you in here. Don't go all girl next door shocked. That's not her."

I nod. "What else?"

"You're shy, she's not. You're a people pleaser, Raelynn doesn't give a fuck. She expects everyone who works for her to be professional, and she compensates them in return. Focus on the job. That's what she'd do. And for heaven's sake, stop saying 'thank you' and 'sorry' to everybody."

"Thanks, Huey." I cover my mouth. "I'm mean, sorry."

He shakes his and leans down close. His eyes leave the room for an instant. "You're not anyone's assistant. You're an A-lister. Act like it."

Huey's right.

It's my mannerisms and demeanor that will screw this up, not my bulging booty. I need to quit being the PA sent to smooth the way for a VIP. Tonight, I am the VIP.

"What's next?" I ask.

"Doug is checking out the VIP area and getting you cleared with club security. Once you're done at the media wall, you'll head over there."

"Fine. Then let's get started."

"Right away, Ms. Tailor."

CHAPTER THREE

WES

"Guys, look this way, please!" a photographer shouts at us as we stand against the media wall. Tonight is huge for Jester's Edge. It's a test of our music, fans, and our relationship with them.

Play. Sing. Write. Perform. None of us are worth a damn doing anything else.

We've known each other since the band started, but what keeps the three of us together is our shared passion and hard work. While me and the guys definitely have our differences, that's one thing we all have in common.

Jai, our bassist, would live in a mud hut if he could still play. Our drummer Vince is a mad-at-the-world type, even when things are damn good, while I'm the glue that holds us together. That and our music.

When I told my bandmates we needed more creative control, the guys agreed to do whatever I thought was best. It's critical that our fanbase identify us with origiality and independence rather than the end-product of a corporate assembly line.

"Wes, Wes. Over here, Wes," several photographers call my name at once.

In exchange for more creative control and higher royalties, Jester's Edge agreed to pay more of our marketing costs. That includes footing the bill for promotional events, music videos, and release parties like this one.

It's a major milestone for us, and it looks like things are going well.

The media wall blazes with our latest album cover. It depicts an idyllic wonderland set against the backdrop of our dystopian world. Not only does it represent an iconic example of semi realism, but it's a fabulous tribute to pop art with our instruments and faces hidden in the background. I've wanted to work with this artist for years, but MaveRICS, our record label, kept shooting me down. Now, this cover's nominated for an industry award.

MaveRICS' own logo appears in an unobtrusive size, relegated to the standard header, right where it belongs. Instead of their brand being on display, our work is front and center, like it should be. After twelve years in this business, good, successful years, I'm getting my way on what's important and matters to me.

It's fucking perfect. Well, almost.

"Raelynn Tailor's arrived," a photographer says. He doesn't shout, but the announcement causes some of them to switch positions. Who can blame them? I'd be lying if I didn't admit to being hyper-tuned in to all things Raelynn Tailor.

From the first 'how's it going? she's had me by the balls, and I've been dying to do something about it.

We met at Food for Thought, a charity which provides meals to poor children over weekends and holidays. We showed up on the same day and someone took pictures of us feeding kids together and posted it on social. Within hours, it went viral, and the fact that we're both single fueled speculation like gasoline and a match.

Soon, both our agents insisted we keep making joint appearances, and it's been an incredible success, boosting Jester's Edge album and ticket sales while giving her huge clout in merchandising ventures.

The truth is that it's all fucking make believe. Damn it.

Whenever we're together, Raelynn's all business and aloof, but then when we text, the warm, funny, and supportive woman is on full display. I don't get it... if she's not interested, why not say so? If she wants to go for a ride, hop on already.

It drives me bat shit crazy.

Through the silent murmurs and stir she creates, I watch as she works the room. Her X-rated, over-the-top costume fits that luscious, toned body like a latex glove. Not only does that sexy mad hatter costume fit the theme of the party and album to perfection, but it also showcases a potent mix of curves, skin, and lace.

She is so... Fucking. Hot.

"Can we get the entire band, please? All of Jester's Edge? Please?" a blur of voices penetrates the chaos.

Beside me, Vince nudges my ribs with his elbow. "Earth to Wes?"

"Sure." I rip my gaze away from Raelynn and face the cameras. "Sure."

After a few more minutes of pictures, the tenor in the room changes as people realize we're both here and wait for us to great each other.

"We should wrap this up, guys." I tell them.

"Go for it," Jai tells me.

"You're already more checked out than a library book." Vince grumbles. "Just don't fuck us up," he says through smiling teeth.

"Vince, it's good for all of us, and you know it," Jai says to him. "We'll see you on stage, Wes."

"Of course."

"Don't fuck us up," Vince warns again.

I hear his warning but ignore it, turning my full attention to Raelynn.

Muted murmurs, sideways glances, and a sudden cessation of attempts to stop or speak with me occur as I make my way across the room. It's like she senses me too. Her back faces me when I approach, but her spine suddenly straightens, and she turns toward me. Behind the Harlequin mask, her intense blue eyes meet mine, and she bites down hard on that blood-red pouty bottom lip.

Fuck. Heat travels down to my knees.

"Angel Eyes." The endearment is out before I can check myself. I don't know where it came from, but it fits her perfectly. "So glad you made it."

"Hello… Wes." She seems detached but not annoyed. That's a plus.

18

I lean down and whisper. "You've got lipstick on your teeth."

"Oh, no." She closes that sensual mouth, smoothing her tongue over the caked red stain. "Better?" she asks.

"Let me." I raise my hand to that come-hither pout and pause for consent.

Beneath the intricate harlequin mask, brilliant blue eyes widen. "Okay."

I rub the pad of my thumb beneath her two front teeth, scraping the blood-red lipstick while her tongue pushes against my intrusion to protect the back of her throat. As I push inside, it strokes against me.

It's official. I'm sprung above and below the waist.

"Is it gone?" she pleads.

I raise my thumb, revealing an unnatural red smear along my thumb pad. "You're good."

"Thank you." She glances over at the red carpet. "How much longer?"

I glance down at my watch where my entire hand now tingles from being in her mouth. "We should hit it soon. They'll let fans outside in at ten."

"Okay," she stands there unmoving.

When she hesitates, I turn and notice her bodyguard watching us with an alert, indecisive scowl.

"Is there a problem?" My gaze shifts between her and the incredible hulk standing beside her.

"None that I'm aware of," he answers after a pause.

"What happens after the photo call?" Angel Eyes interrupts our exchange.

"We can mingle inside the club for a while before heading to the VIP lounge."

"Who's in there?" she asks.

"Right now, friends, family and industry people. It won't take long, and getting pics with some of them is great exposure for everyone."

"Should I take my security team with me?" She glances over at her bodyguard.

"I don't think so." I glance back at him. "Is something going on you want to tell me about?"

"Not at all," he reassures me. "Ms. Tailor, Doug and I will remain on the premises close by. We've worked with the band's security before, so the lounge area is fine." His voice drops. "You can text me if you need anything."

She nods at him in confirmation.

"Come on. Let's get going," she tells me with a reassuring smile.

As we walk the red carpet together, it's a genuine struggle to keep my eyes off her. Tonight, she's pleasant and professional as ever, but she doesn't own the photo call like she usually does. The supermodel I work with owns any walkway she cares to grace. Photographers don't tell her to pose, they go with what she gives them.

"Are you okay?" I ask.

"Fine," she replies. "Sorry."

Maybe she's trying not to steal the band's thunder? For the next few minutes, both of us take direction from the photographers.

"Lots of smiles!"

"Closer, please!"

"Over here, please!"

Everything's going great, we're almost finished, when

someone yelps out the question I've been dying for and dreading at the same time.

"Huge night! Where's the big kiss?"

We're supposed to be a couple, so this isn't a surprise. In the course of our careers, we've both done this a million times before, ourselves and with other people. Determined to keep things professional, I move the same way as always when we work together.

"You ready, Angel Eyes?" I whisper as she turns toward me.

She responds with a nod, and I place both hands high on the sides of her waist. Staring at the space between the painted eyebrows on her mask, I aim for the corner of her mouth away from the photographers and make contact.

Only this time, something unexpected happens.

Instead of puckering and turning at an angle to create an illusion of touch, she presses her mouth on mine. Those hot, pouty, warm, wet, red lips capture me in their torturous grasp.

For a split second, I assume one of us made a mistake. But when I attempt to pull away, my lower lip gets caught between hers as she holds them together.

Holy Shit. That's no accident.

My eyes fly open to study hers. Shut tight behind the harlequin mask, they reveal nothing. But the curve of her cheek, the tilt of her chin, and the smudged lipstick tell me she's living in this moment. It's real for her. And for me. She's flipped the script, big-time.

Un-fucking believable.

Of all the places to come clean about her feelings, it had to be here? Now? For months, I've struggled to remain in park around her. Compliments met with impatient eye rolls. Invitations rejected because of dubious plans. Questions about her work answered with minimal amounts of civility and information. The hell of it is, I got the message loud and clear. It stung like a bitch, but I respected her boundaries, even though her texts sent different signals.

The sounds of claps, catcalls, and cameras clicking call me back to reality. My fingers caress her jawbone as I pull away, and her eyes fly wide open. Her expression is a mix of shock and disbelief, heat and hunger. This is the biggest night of my life, but right now I don't want to be anywhere but alone with her.

"You okay, Angel Eyes?"

She nods but doesn't speak. She struggles to pull it together, but she can't quite nail it. Maybe it's the excitement and the energy that surrounds us. Some people find it an arousing aphrodisiac. It is for me. After a fantastic live performance, all I want to do is fuck. No Booze, no drugs, just sex until my balls ache.

It's also possible that she's had too much going on in her life and wasn't interested in start anything new. It's spring now, and the major fashion weeks don't occur until fall.

From the media wall, I scan the room, then glance back down at her. She's nervous, shaken, and doing her best to look like she gives a fuck.

This is a huge night for us, but I've got to make a choice. Sort this out with her now or bury it for good. Because if I don't talk to her alone and figure out once and for all what the hell is going on, she'll find an excuse to blow the whole thing off.

Damn if I'll let that happen.

"You want to get out here?" Fuck. I can't believe I just said that. I can't believe I meant it.

"God yes." She rasps.

When I reach over and squeeze her hand, she squeezes back. That's all it takes.

"Thanks everyone." I announce to the photographers before leaving the media wall with my hand pressed against her hip.

"Come with me." I don't ask.

CHAPTER FOUR

ROSE

*W*hat the hell just happened?

One minute we're doing the photo call, the next we're kissing. For real. Mind blowing. Panty melting. Life changing.

All I remember were his lips near mine and he was pulling me close and the thought that went through my mind was 'I'll never get another chance to kiss him.'

So, I did. Stupid. Foolish. Crazy.

He hurries us away from the media wall into the main area of the club with heated impatience. It's almost impossible for me to keep up with him in these stiletto heels while this thong rides up my ass.

"Wes!" I place my hand over his where he holds my arm and pull back.

He stops and looks at me but doesn't speak.

"That… what we did back there, um… It shouldn't have happened. It was my mistake, and I'm sorry," I stammer.

He laughs but sounds unamused. "Yeah, I figured you'd say something like that. Not buying it."

"Well, I'm not selling anything." I pull free from his grasp. "Time for me to go now." It hurts to admit the truth sometimes, but there it is.

This world belongs to my sister, not me. As identical twins, our individual identities are a touchstone issue. I've spent so much of my life trying to carve out an existence separate from my famous, super-successful twin that this —the club, the costume, the make-up—feels… perverse.

And as I stand here face to face with one of the top recording artists today, it occurs to me that Sergio isn't the only reason Raelynn didn't want to show up tonight.

I'm a professional musician too. Or was once upon a time.

Maybe an album launch party felt too much like me and not enough like her.

"Answer a question for me first," Wes says, interrupting my thoughts. "Was what you did back there some kind of stunt?"

"Stunt?" I blink.

"Yeah. Remember when I won the award for best male vocalist and you stained my cheek with your poppies-in-winter lip gloss? Or the time we attended the Grand Gala and I helped wrangle your dress wearing the latest Tissot watch? You know, a stunt."

I should lie and make something up. Lord knows I've

told some whoppers on behalf of other people, but that's not how things work in my personal life.

"No." I swallow hard. "It wasn't a stunt."

Wes licks his lips, faces me, and wraps his arms around my waist. He looks down at me with intense, black-lashed, green eyes. "You kissed me. I want an explanation. You owe me that much."

"There's nothing to explain." My nervous laughter falls flat. "Maybe I was just curious and now I'm over it."

"Curious?" His eyebrows raise at the word. "Isn't that sweet? Guess what? I'm curious, too. And far from over it. Let's go."

"Where?"

"Some place we can be alone for a few minutes."

Shit.

How well does he know my sister? Up close, will he realize I'm not her? People who know us are aware Raelynn has a sister, but only a few know we're identical twins. She doesn't like to broadcast it, because she wants me to pull stunts like this without arousing suspicion, damn it.

We're the same height, five-nine, but possess obvious physical differences. Our natural hair color is walnut brown, but she keeps hers blonde for modelling. I wear glasses while Rae had LASIK years ago. With careful dieting and a stable of experts, my famous sister is a size two, while I'm a six on an extremely good day.

If Wes picks up on any of this, what will he do about their contract? Rumor has it he's becoming a music mogul of his era. A prodigious artist with incredible business sense and understanding of the music industry. Translation

—not someone you want to face off against in a contractual dispute.

"Let's make a deal," he says after a few minutes. "You come with me right now, and you're done with PR for the night. You won't have to fake another smile or take anymore pictures."

"Promise?"

"Promise."

There's not much choice. The longer I stay here the greater risk of being discovered. At least I'll only need to convince one person I'm Raelynn instead of a hundred. Besides, Wes doesn't have much time. They're in the middle of the launch party and he's got things to do.

"Okay," I sigh. "Let's hurry though. Please?"

"As you wish."

Wes's firm, warm hand encircles my naked waist, pulling me closer as he picks up the pace. Dumbstruck, I let him lead me to HotZone's main level.

It's huge.

Two large bars run along the sides of the dance floor, each with seating for forty. Another fifteen tables surround them, separated from the main floor by metal rails.

The sheer size overwhelms me, and the decor is mind blowing. The room screams dystopian children's story. Glowing mason jars decorate the tables, while gritty subway maps and oversized posters of Jester's Edge adorn the walls.

There are at least three hundred costumed partiers here. Sexy kitties, X-rated bunnies, playing card royalty, all talking, drinking, dancing to the audio remixes of the band's songs.

As Wes hurries me along, I resist the urge to clutch his waist and coil my fingers through the belt loop of his pants instead. He responds by pulling me closer, which causes his long dark trench coat to drape around my shoulders.

That's when I get a good look at his costume.

Those snug, leather, lace-up jeans are standard issue for a rocker at work, while the sheer mesh fabric of his shirt displays his sculpted chest and abs, along with an impressive collection of tattoos, including a big red heart that stands out among the rest.

"Who are you supposed to be?" I stare into black-lashed green eyes.

"Knave of Hearts," he answers with a heated grin. "Who else?"

In the children's book, the Knave of Hearts stood trial for stealing from the Queen. Standing here right now, he's the perfect embodiment of a fantasy character come to life.

As he leads me deeper into the club, people recognize him. They do double-takes, point him out, even clap.

"Great launch party!"

"Congratulations, Wes!"

"Love the outfit!"

Wes nods and smiles but doesn't slow down. Instead, he fumbles with something around his head and pulls it down onto his face, which elicits oohs and applause from a small group.

When he looks down at me, there's a big red heart emblazoned on the patch that covers his left eye.

Damn, I couldn't make this up.

A pair of large men wearing Jester's Edge T-shirts stand next to the staircase that runs perpendicular to the stage. Wes nods at them and one man removes the chain across the railing with a sign that reads 'VIP LOUNGE.'

Ahead of me, Wes's heavy boots create a dull thud as he jogs upstairs while I remain at the bottom. Metallic perforations on the industrial steps present a perfect, dangerous trap for my stiletto heels.

"What's wrong?" Wes asks.

"These stairs." My index finger points downward. "I'll need to take this slow."

Testing my boot on the stair, my slender heel fits perfectly into one of the metallic oval holes. It wedges inside and I battle to pull it out. It doesn't help that my mask and crazy oversized hat make it difficult to see when I look down.

"Angel Eyes, we don't have time for this," he grumbles.

Wes races down the stairs, and with unexpected speed releases my boot with a single tug.

"Thank- yow!" I gasp as he lifts my body up and upends me over his shoulder.

"Hey!" I shriek. "What are you doing?"

"Protecting you." His voice is playful, but his grip on my legs and torso tightens. "And those sexy fuck-me boots."

Wes strokes the back of my thighs, eliciting a tense breath from me. I can't tell if it's meant to be protective or tantalizing, but I arch in response, which dislodges my heavily weighted velvet hat, causing me pain as it tears the wig cap that secures it to my head.

Against the top ridge of his shoulder, my pelvis curves into him, trying to keep my balance and prevent more damage to my scalp. Being held upside down was not a scenario Rae or I envisioned when she pinned the wig cap to my hair and glued the hat to my slip band.

"Easy, gorgeous, or we'll both have a tumble. Before we're ready." He gives my ass a firm, playful slap.

What the hell?

"Who you with there, Wes?" someone from the throng below shouts.

"Don't you dare," I warn him between gritted teeth before he answers.

"Why not?" he asks. "They know who you are—or will figure it out fast enough. Say hello." He shifts me toward the crowd.

"We're done here." I answer with assertive calm. "Let me down so I can leave."

His head turns sideways to look at me. Not even my mask can disguise the bitch-face I'm giving him.

"You made me a promise," he insists.

"To talk in private." I remind him. "I didn't agree to this."

"Relax, and have a little fun," he tells me. "It is a party, you know."

I bite my lip, hard, and peer at the dance floor, milling with people watching us. "Just… enough, okay?"

He winks at me and gestures toward his fans. "Sorry, guys. I'm keeping this one to myself."

His announcement causes laughter mixed with coarse comments, some lewd jokes, and a healthy dose of boos. I'm ready to breathe a sigh of relief and thank him, but before that happens, he slaps my ass again, then plants a loud wet kiss on my exposed butt cheek bent across his shoulder.

Not even the roar of his fans can mute the clank of his rapid ascent up the metal stairs or the angry sound of the blood rushing to my head.

CHAPTER FIVE

WES

"Wes," she warns me.

"Relax, Angel eyes. Almost there."

As I climb the stairs, she arches her neck and holds the brim of that silly ass hat to stop it from falling off, sucking in several pain-filled breaths along the way. Her breasts slam into my shoulders with each step, creating a special brand of slow, exquisite torture. As I steady my pace to spare her further hurt, my own impatient agony spikes.

"For the next twenty minutes, you haven't seen me," I tell my regular bodyguard who's stationed at the entrance of the VIP lounge at the top of the stairs.

Greg nods, then hustles ahead of me. A small group of people mingle up here, but they're too into their own thing to pay much notice us hurrying by them.

Greg reaches the gray painted metal door a few moments before I do and pushes it open just as I arrive. We exchange a knowing glance before it shuts behind me.

"Put me down. Please." Her plea is intense, insistent.

I loosen my grip and she slides down my torso, holding steady as every taunt inch of her grinds against me until she finds her footing.

God, that feels nice.

As she stands up, I find my hands resting on the cheeks of her incredible ass. I let myself drown in those ice-blue eyes, which stare, mesmerized, into mine.

"Alone." I breathe a sigh of relief, then bend close for a kiss.

She grabs my biceps, one in each hand, while her entire body stills. Beneath the Harlequin mask, that hypnotic gaze emits eager desire. That's the last thing I see before my lips reach that sensual mouth, and...

"Please. Don't," she says, turning away.

"What?" I stroke her shoulder as she gazes at me.

"Did you spank my ass? In front of all those people?" She pushes against my chest and swings away.

I jerk back and our eyes clash. "Um, I kissed it, too. Remember?"

She responds with a death glare, and it registers that she's pissed off. Super pissed.

"Okay, I'm sorry. It was firm, fine, perfect, and it got a little hot." I offer her an apologetic smile.

"That's not the point." She withdraws from my touch and steps back, pacing down the long length of the L-shaped couch. A large flat screen television hangs on the largest wall. Across from it, a smaller cluster of CCTVs allows us to watch the club action from here.

"I said I was sorry, but don't turn me into the bad guy here," I tell her from the other side of the couch. "You came here, dressed like that, and you kissed me at the photo call. Now you're complaining about too much attention?" I laugh in disbelief, then stop short when she scowls at me. "Since when?"

"Now."

From the minute she sauntered into the club, subdued, sexy, aloof, she's radiated irresistible allure. Tonight, the fun-loving model who enjoys being the center of the universe remains missing in action.

This quiet, sultry, pouty version is much more potent.

"Be careful, Angel Eyes. I will not let you pretend you're clueless about how I feel after this. It's the reason I wanted you to come up here and talk."

"Feelings? Please. This is a big night for you, and we both got caught up in the moment."

"Bullshit. I've been coming on to you for months."

Her eyes widen and she turns away. "That's—"

"What? Tell me," I ask, crossing the room to stand next to her. "For months, we've been going round and round. Tonight I told myself to behave around you, keep things professional."

"Spanking me on the staircase in front of a crowd is keeping things professional?"

"I could say the same about you kissing me for real in the middle of a photo call."

"Maybe it is my costume." She peers down at her exposed cleavage and yanks the sides of the barely there bustier. "Being dressed like this… being incognito, I'm acting in ways I normally wouldn't."

"Whatever. Fuck the suit. If you need an excuse to explore your true feelings, that's fine with me."

"Wes," she stammers. "Haven't you ever gotten carried away?"

"At a work gig? With someone I wasn't interested in?" I stare straight at her without blinking. "No. Never."

"I don't believe it."

"Really? At all of our joint appearance, I've come on to you. I'd given up until tonight's kiss." I brace my hands on both sides of her waist while she looks up at me. My chin rests against the top of her head. "Thank you for changing your mind."

"Is that what you think happened?"

"Didn't it? Whenever I became convinced that you weren't interested, we'd end up texting one more time." I press my lips to her forehead at the memory. "You were always kind, supportive, funny… whatever I needed. It gave me hope that you'd give us a chance someday. And I was right."

"I'm not sure about that," she sputters in disbelief.

"I am. It makes perfect sense. People proposition you every day. It happens to me too. But neither one of us had the bandwidth to sort it out at the time. But now that we've released the album and the major fashion weeks are a long way off, we can give it a try."

She stares at nothing for a few moments, then faces me. Her expression radiates with a rainbow of naked emotions. Attraction. Regret. Disappointment. A single tear forms, but she brushes it aside before it falls.

"Please." Her voice is hoarse. "I lack the strength to say no to you."

"I knew it." My chest swells with elation. "You've been holding back too. How long?"

"A while," she admits. "But it's not what you think."

"Yeah, never mixing business with pleasure is one of my rules too," I confess. "We both fucked up a little in that department." I swallow hard before speaking. "But we need to give this a chance. Keeping this quiet works for me. Fuck the contract."

I know she needs time and space to digest my words, so I take my time, slowly removing my trench coat and eye patch before tossing them on the sectional to fill the strained silence.

When the sound of the leather slaps against the chair, she startles and faces me.

She breaks eye contact and studies my tattoos through the thin mesh of my shirt. Her face flushes pink as she takes an unsteady seat on the couch's backrest, crossing those endless legs together so tight I can see the elongated muscles of her outer thighs twitch.

"Give me a chance. Please," I whisper.

My lips find the soft curve of her shoulder where I blow, nibble, and suck the delicate, responsive flesh.

"Uh…" she bites her lip.

Our mouths collide in an urgent tangle of taste, teeth, and tongues, her excitement a match for my own. My hand slides from the top of that perfect heart-shaped ass, along the exposed sensual skin of her curved spine, pulling her closer to me.

"Yes or no?" I push. Being in limbo with her makes me ache, and I'm rapidly reaching a point of no return.

"What if I'm not the person you think I am or want me to be? Because believe me, I'm not."

"I know all I need to know about you right now." He caresses my cheek. "I'm crazy about you, and the feeling is mutual."

"What if this turns out to be a terrible mistake?"

"It's not." I nuzzle the nape of her neck.

"Don't hurt me, okay?" she asks in a way that suggests she doesn't mean physically.

"Never," I promise. "We're alone here. Greg's outside is my security guy. He won't let anyone inside."

A flash of… something radiates from her eyes.

Then she nods twice and molds herself to me. Hips arched, legs wrapped around my waist. Without another word, I hold her thighs tight against me, step over the backrest and lay her down on the padded cushions beneath me.

CHAPTER SIX

ROSE

Our hands are everywhere, which is a good thing because it keeps me from thinking too much. I tried my best to warn and dissuade him, but I'm only human, and he's not wrong.

I've been crazy about him for months.

Not in a groupie worshipper sort of way, but as someone who got to know him on a personal level and liked what I discovered. Being Raelynn's assistant has made me an expert on dealing with demanding divas. Believe me, the glitter fades fast. Wes Anders might not suffer fools, but he's a genuine artist and a gentleman to the little people.

When I reach under his mesh shirt to trace the tattoos

that have taunted and tantalized me all evening, my doubts disappear.

Wes's lips are full and tender, the polar opposite of the five o'clock shadow that scrapes my cheek and chin, heightening my awareness of him. The potent scents of citrus, cedar, and heat overwhelm me, and I become pliant under his weight.

As he burrows between my legs and turns my body, we sink into the soft couch cushions. The pads of my fingers explore the ridges of his abs and pecs, eliciting a throaty groan from him I both feel and hear.

Through the flimsy fabric of my bustier and thong, we share all the shameless friction of every contortion. The flexing of his arms. The tightening of my nipples. The arch of my pelvis. The swelling of his groin.

A swirl of physical and emotional sensations blend into one. I think we're both overwhelmed when he sits backs on his heels and stares at me for a few seconds.

"You're so lucky I brought you up here." He smirks, breathless.

"Did you just congratulate yourself?"

"Hell, yeah." His grin reminds me of a Cheshire Cat. "This costume is a fucking turn on." His flat palms run up from my waist to below my breasts.

"Well, I'm glad it works for you."

"You should be. You think I'd be the only man all over you, looking like this?"

"Do you expect a 'thank you?'" I ask, incredulous.

"It's a close second to hero worship." He hesitates a moment. "But I'll leave it up to you."

"Up to me? What was your back-up plan, a game of cards?"

Wes shrugs. "I'm always ready for a few hands of strip poker," he offers with that boy-next-door smile.

I laugh. "You'd never collect. A team of experts poured me into this."

"Really? Well, it looks like it's up to this expert to get you out of it."

"Easier said than done," I warn him.

My specialties include tucking and taping my sister into outfits with impossible plunges and minimal coverage while allowing movement and minimizing wardrobe malfunctions. Tonight marked a rare time that Raelynn helped me dress for an event.

The realization brings the horror of my current situation front and center. How the hell will I get dressed without seriously skilled help?

"Don't worry. You can wear my trench coat." It's like he's read my mind.

"What about you?" I point toward the sheer mesh shirt that displays an impressive mix of tattoos and muscular ridges. "That's… quite a display."

"Forget it. All in a day's work." Wes runs eager hands over the length of my body. Touching, testing, tugging as he inspects the lace, clasps, and ties of my costume.

"Is this a corset?"

"Yes…"

"That means the panties aren't attached, right?"

"Right."

"And you need to loosen the laces along the back before you can unbutton the front?" he confirms.

"Um, correct."

He snaps the waist of my thong and gives me a wicked smile. "Lucky me. Take your topcoat off. Leave the rest to me."

"Everything?"

"Trust me, I got this."

His confident expertise on the subject of removing women's lingerie startles me a bit. But that doesn't stop me from scrambling to my feet and standing behind the armrest to strip out of my topcoat, which will take longer than he realizes.

Surgical-strength tape fastens the topcoat to my skin to prevent wardrobe malfunctions. Starting at my clavicle, several dozen individual pieces hold the long coat collar in place, from the barely there straps of my bodice down and alongside my cleavage, where it protects against spillage.

The industrial stickiness hurts when I pull it off too fast. Its harsh sensation causes me to wince, whimper, and jiggle with every painstaking inch removed. I'm twisting my breast out of its corset to yank off the tape when I hear delighted groans from the far side of the couch.

"Don't stop, Angel Eyes," he growls. "You're fucking mind blowing."

One hand props up his head, those long, sculpted fingers partly concealing his mouth and eyes from view, while the other fumbles with the cords of his lace-up pants.

His feral, heated gaze makes me conscious of my own movements. As I turn to face him, my now un-taped jacket drapes off my shoulder like a shawl, exposing the naked skin of my arms and the unrestrained spillage of my breast.

"Don't stop," he tells me again, untying the lace-up fly on his leather pants before sliding them down past his hips. "Your naughty striptease is milestone birthday awesome."

"Is it your birthday?" I ask.

"Nope." He licks his lips. "But your number one on my invite list."

"Good to know." My laugh is breathless and raspy.

Wes's eagerness awakens my naughtiness. I'm conscious of his gaze on me as I tear the wardrobe tape from my other shoulder, down the side of my breast to where it secures the coat along the waist of my thong.

Sheer lace hugs the exposed curve of the cheek he spanked earlier tonight, and I moan softly while I caress the red mark it left. Behind me, more restless movement and impatient moans erupt from the couch.

The topcoat drapes off my shoulders, exposing the ties of my corset. Through it all, I'm conscious of his eyes on me, of every move I make, and my shameless attempts to turn him on. By the time it glides down my arms, Wes is beside me, kissing my naked shoulder.

"I can't wait anymore," he whispers, tossing my topcoat to the floor.

His lips descend to the arc of my shoulder. As he presses into me, his smooth skin slides against mine, and I realize he's removed his shirt. Those sculpted hands settle on my waist, pulling me close, before he explores the lace ties that run along the back of my corset. The rustle of ribbon as it whips through metal eyelets is the only sound in the still, heated atmosphere of the private room.

"Don't worry, I'll take good care of you," he promises between gentle nibbles on my earlobe.

I draw a deep breath and feel strong musicians' hands curve around the small of my back, his fingers intertwining with the laces he finds there. With a single, powerful flex of both wrists, he releases the tension on them.

"Oh!" I gasp.

"We're good," he says with a hint of laughter. "Still wearable."

Wes coils one arm around me and works the hook-and-eye closures on the front of my corset. One handed (one fucking handed!) he unfastens them, freeing my breasts from their tight constraints. I groan and turn toward him, the skin of our heated bodies flesh-to-flesh.

His eager mouth wastes no time taunting, tasting, and teasing my nipples with his tongue. He pushes me against the back of the couch and my weighted hat pulls the hair out by the roots as my neck arches back. I try to ignore the pain, but Wes notices my struggle.

"Damn it." I fumble with my hat and curse between rapid breaths.

"Can we get this off?" He urges, holding the brim.

"Unless I tear out huge chunks of my scalp, this will take a while."

"That's too fucking slow, and I don't want you hurt. We'll think of something else."

He studies the large gray sectional we're leaning against. Grabbing my legs from around his waist he positions me over the backrest. With a quick leap, he jumps over, then slides me down onto the couch.

"Try this." He crushes the brim against the armrest and cradles the crook of my neck along the curve, so it supports the oppressive weight of my hat.

"Good?" He caresses my face in a tender, unexpected gesture.

"Mmm."

He looks at me under him. My corset is open, exposing my torso to his gaze, which lingers on the waist of my thong. Wes goes to work peeling it down to the middle of my thighs, then settles himself between my legs.

"Love these fuck me boots." He pulls one up to his face and drops a kiss on my ankle before hooking it over his shoulder. "You won't regret wearing them tonight," he says.

Wes pops a finger in his mouth, then traces a line down my exposed center strip. One, two, then three fingers take their time, delving inside my slick, achy folds.

My hips writhe at the intrusion, wanting so much more than his fingers.

"You like when I touch you there?" he asks.

"Mmm," I agree, and he pushes deep into me again.

He strokes me with one hand, then kisses my other ankle and hooks it over his other shoulder, inching my exposed swollen folds toward the tip of his hard, heated cock. I'm breathless, impatient, ready for him.

He gives me a knowing smile as he breaks eye contact

to pull a condom from the leather jeans crumpled beside him.

"Look at me," he demands. "I want to watch you."

Our eyes meet and my gaze doesn't waver, partly because he asked, but mostly because I need to watch him too. Wes grabs the tops of my upper thighs and positions my entrance against his throbbing erection. My hands dig into the cushions as I raise my hips in anticipation.

"Look at you," he whispers as he rolls on a condom.

"Right back at you." I slide my swollen folds across his bulbous crown.

"You good?" he asks, breathless.

"Just fine. Could be better, though." I bite my lip, the way I now realize excites him.

"Well, okay then."

He grips my thighs again, and with a single deep plunge, impales himself inside me with a loud, feral groan.

"Christ, I've needed to be inside you for so fucking long." He pants while my own cries resonate with need, pleasure, and satisfaction.

Wes lifts my pelvis again, raising me to the tip of his hardened length before plunging in again. He does this over and over, until I measure time by the rhythm of our strokes. As the flesh of his shoulders grows slick with sweat, my ankle slides down his arm. Fearful of being unjoined, I put my leg on the couch and inch myself closer to him.

Holding my other leg in place, he hooks it up onto his shoulder, grips my opposite hip, and grinds against *that* spot with gratifying precision.

My hips writhe and rise off the couch, but he pins me down, leaving me no escape from our heated friction. It melts my insides, paving the way for a monstrous release coming at me with the force of a freight train.

"Right there," he begs. My tight channel throbs and pulses around his engorged length. "Don't fight it." His voice is jagged, breathless.

Wes's face is a perfect mixture of distracted bliss and intense concentration as he pummels away with feral fervor that's emotional and physical for both of us. His deep deliberate thrusts send me past my limits in no time.

My orgasm renders me speechless. The only sounds I make are groans of pleasure.

He strokes faster, deeper, until I feel his own release build before it explodes. We crest together and his own climax amplifies and extends my own.

"So good. Come for me, Raelynn."

I stare up at his face, and he looks down at me with a sensual expression through long, thick lashes. Then his body bows into mine, he throws his head back and groans as he shudders, rocking us both to our cores.

Tears pool in the bottom of my mask as I surrender to the most satisfying, heartbreaking orgasm of my entire life.

But did he need to scream my sister's name like that?

CHAPTER SEVEN

WES

My body falls against hers onto the plush couch cushions. With my front to her back, I curl my naked frame around her pliant form and throw my arm across her. I'm already hard again, and it's tempting to coax her into another round.

But a different part of me wants to savor the gratification that follows great sex. These are the first few precious moments of peace and satisfaction I've enjoyed in months.

Sex tonight was an anomaly. It sure as hell wasn't a natural progression of our current relationship. Hell, we hadn't even exchanged an unscripted kiss until thirty minutes ago.

But it wasn't a fast and furious fling between strangers

looking for a quickie with no chance of seeing each other again either.

Fuck buddies? We're not exactly friends. We seem to get along well when we text, but except for tonight, our in-person encounters are painfully impersonal. Instead, it was sudden, spontaneous, a more... primal, physical connection.

Beside me, she shivers.

"Cold?" I hobble on my knees to the far side of the couch, retrieve my leather jacket, and drape it over her body. She responds with a whimper.

"Are you okay?" I ask.

She doesn't speak, merely moves her head. That stupid hat is still on, which must be uncomfortable. I can't get her to answer, but ignoring her discomfort is impossible. Since I don't know what to say, I do what comes naturally when words fail me.

I turn to music.

After planting a soft kiss on her shoulder, I begin to hum. It's an older melody from my teens that I'd work on when no one close to me understood how I felt.

Next to me, her body relaxes, and she sighs a few times as I continue. After a few moments, she stuns me my humming along. As she adds her own improvisations, I stop and listen to her raspy, deep, emotional tone as she alters the original melody.

"Do you sing, Angel eyes?" I ask when she stops.

Before she can answer, the sound of voices in the hallway shatters our private cocoon.

"Like I give a fuck, Greg. We were supposed to start

our set almost an hour ago. A fucking hour! Get out of my way. Yeah, I know what he's doing."

Fuck. My body goes from relaxed to rigid and my forehead droops against the small of her back.

Beside me, Angel Eyes drapes my leather jacket over her naked breasts and sits up. When someone pounds on the door, her spine stiffens.

"Anders!" I recognize Vince's voice. *"Wes!"*

"Fuck," I mutter before slapping my cheeks a few times to help me focus.

"Yeah, Vince."

"You're late. Let's go," he shouts.

"Be right there," I growl, unable to hide my annoyance. At him. At myself.

There's a single loud bang that sounds as if someone punched the door, more muffled conversation, and then we're alone again.

To say that I lost track of time in her arms is a damn understatement. Of course I'd remembered the set we planned to play, and thinking it would be a late start. But a fucking hour late with no heads up to the guys makes me the asshole in this situation.

Beside me, she scoots herself to the opposite side and stands, all without a single glance in my direction.

"Angel Eyes, I am so sorry, but I've got to leave."

"No problem." Her voice cracks.

"Are you okay?" I ask.

She nods but doesn't speak, so I move to other side of the couch and face her. Tears seep through the bottom of her mask, and she wipes them with an angry gesture.

"Fuck. Fuck!" I rake my finger through my hair and pull the ends until it hurts. "Please don't do this."

"Do what?" she snaps.

Startled, I take her hand and kiss it.

"Be mad. Or feel mistreated." I watch the base of her throat as she swallows. "I'm not this big of a selfish asshole. Truth."

"You should leave," she tells me, clutching my jacket to her chest.

"Ah, shit." My hands cup her wet face. "This is not how I wanted this to go."

"Maybe we should've stuck to that game of strip poker."

I humph in response, then kneel on the couch's armrest and take both her hands in mine.

"Look at me. If I had known there was a snowball's chance in hell that we would end up like this tonight," my voice cracks, "Christ."

"Don't worry about it." Her body starts to sway.

"I wanted our first time together to be so much better than this." I run a hand through my hair.

"Sorry to disappoint you." Her bitterness comes through loud and clear.

"Hold on a second." I pull her close to me. "That's not what I meant and you know it. Please don't do this."

"It's okay. Really," she insists.

"Like hell it is. Let me make this up to you," I plead. "Come home with me. We'll have a do-over. I'll cook you breakfast, treat you right."

When she shakes her head, tears seep out the sides and slits of her mask. "I'll… think about it."

You're losing her.

"Well, at least come down and watch the show." I give her my best sincere smile. "I know a guy who'll find you a great seat."

"I'm sure you do." Her laughter is filled with sadness. "I should get dressed. Can you give me some time?"

"Anything for you." I plant a hurried kiss on her lips. "See you downstairs."

I pull my pants over my hips and head for the door. As it shuts behind me, the feeling that I've fucked up becomes more unshakable with each step I take toward the stage and away from her.

CHAPTER EIGHT

ROSE

*W*es wrestling his bare ass cheeks into tight leather pants as he raced like a bat out of hell from the scene of our hookup etches itself into my memory before I collapse back onto the couch and stare at the ceiling.

He called me Angel Eyes. Just like he did that night.

Wes and Raelynn had planned to make a joint public appearance at the Musician of the Year Awards. The major event threw the entire household into a tizzy, and everyone needed to concentrate on getting her ready, which was why the incessant commotion on the porch went unanswered.

Rae's screeching about her makeup ceased long enough for a colossal meltdown about the obnoxious doorbell chimes. Frustrated, I ran downstairs to answer it myself, intent on chewing out the limo driver.

Did he think we'd forgotten about tonight? I yanked open the door, set to give him hell. Instead, I choked on my tongue.

Wes Anders stood on the porch. Dressed to impress, his tall, fit body leaned against the door frame. The dark maroon suit with black pinstripes was a radical departure from his trademark silk tee shirts, leather pants, and five hundred-dollar sneakers. He wore a black dress shirt with a Neryu collar that shimmered in the early evening sunlight, an exact match for his shiny, jet-black hair.

"Hello." His full lips radiated with a boy-next-door smile that revealed straight white teeth.

"Ca- ca, can I help you?" I stammered like an incoherent moron.

When his gaze raked me up and down, I drew a shocked breath and creamed my panties. It was the best and worst moment of my life. Here he was, booted and suited in lady killer style, standing in front of me. Looking at me with those black-lashed cat green eyes, smiling at me with those full lips and sensual mouth.

And there I was…

My weight was at an all-time high, a solid thirty pounds more than I am right now. I'm a stress eater, and there was a lot of pressure in my life back then. The gray yoga pants and pale pink satin baseball jacket I'd pulled wrinkled from the clothes dryer that morning did nothing to hide it.

Large, dark-rimmed glasses overwhelmed my face, making me resemble an enormous owl, and an unkempt knot of unwashed chestnut brown hair teetered on my head.

But that wasn't the worst of it.

Secured to the top of my messy bun was a pin cushion embellished with needles strung with lengths of various colored threads and an extensive selection of safety pins that served as Raelynn's wardrobe malfunction antidote. An iPad stylus and blue sharpies for autographs fanned out between coiled strands of hair, keeping my hands free for other tasks.

I looked like a Grand Ole Opry comedian, only more comical. Humiliation and embarrassment seethed inside me.

"Do we know each other, Angel Eyes?" Wes cocked his head to the side and studied my face.

"No," I answered in a short tone. Despite my drab appearance, I still bore a resemblance to my twin, something I'd been struggling to distance myself from since high school.

"Too bad." He smiled again.

"Do you want to wait inside? Raelynn isn't ready yet."

"Total shocker. Total," he replied. "I'll come in if you promise to keep me company."

Why is he fucking with me? I wondered.

"Me?" I replied. "Why me?"

"You just seem like good company." He shrugged. "You work for Raelynn?"

That's it. He wants the 4-1-1 on my sister. Not happening, Rockstar.

"Obviously." I smiled.

"Are you her assistant?" he asked.

"Something like that. Would you like a drink or a snack?"

"No, thank you. I can't eat before these things." He entered the foyer. "Nothing stays down. Speaking of nerves, can I ask you a favor?"

My throat felt like I was swallowing wet cement. "What is it?"

He stepped close to me and snaked his long fingers up near his neck, where they twisted a loose button. "Between being nervous about tonight and this shirt irritating the hell out of me, I pulled this off." Wes dangled it from a thin thread. "Are you any good with that arsenal?" His chin jutted toward the pin cushion tangled in my hair. "Can you fix me up?"

As I reached over to take it, his hand extended out to me, and our fingers collided. A jolt of... something shot through me, and I'd hoped to hell he didn't notice the sudden rise in my body temperature.

"Did you feel that?" he asked.

"What do you mean?"

"That spark? When I touched you."

"Um, yeah." I shifted, uncomfortable discussing it. "Sorry. It must be from running on the upstairs carpet." I tear my eyes away from his and concentrate on his button. "Do you still want me to sew this?"

"Please. I don't wear ties, and if this shirt comes open, I'll look like shit."

"No, you won't," I insisted. "But I can fix it anyway."

I grabbed a pre-threaded needle from my pin cushion and moved closer. He leaned down over me and watched as I brought it close to his throat. His breathing, low and even, emitted a mint scent laced with the faintest trace of whiskey.

When I slipped my hand underneath his shirt to pull the needle through, my fingers brushed the smooth bare skin of his toned, muscular chest. The fabric fluttered with my movements, and after a few passes through the button's holes, a potent knee weakening whiff of him overwhelmed my senses.

He smelled like soap, citrus, cedarwood... and heat.

Determined to avoid eye contact, I fixated on the base of his collar bone as he swallowed hard several times. Distracted, I pricked myself, but hardly noticed the pain.

"Finished?" he asked.

"Just about." I knotted the thread inside the shirt, then wrapped it around the back of the button. I leaned in close again to cut the excess with the scissors hanging from my neck. "There."

"Great." His fingers tested it with a gentle tug, then he bent down and whispered, "Wonder Woman to the rescue. Thanks."

"You're welcome."

When I looked up at him, his eyes filled with mischief, curiosity, challenge.

"I'm Wes," he said after a long pause.

"It's nice to meet you," I replied.

Those were the last words we exchanged. Moments

later, Raelynn descended, every inch the goddess, and everyone refocused their attention on her.

I never got the chance to tell him my name.

Maybe I'd hoped that he'd realize it was me, the frazzled assistant who sewed his button back on while he joked about sparks between us. The entire time tonight, he never called me anything but Angel Eyes, until the moment of our mutual climax.

My eyes clench tight at the memory.

Get up.

My feet snake their way to the floor, and I force myself to sit up. As I scan the private room, a sigh of relief escapes me when I notice an ajar door in the far corner. Thank heaven it's a bathroom. Despite being alone, I shut the tiny door with a firm thud and lock it behind me. Then I lift my mask onto the brim of my asinine hat and deal with the makeup meltdown underneath.

This disaster is mine to own because I came here pretending to be my twin sister, and voila! Success. Go team Rosalie.

This isn't Wes's fault. And this entire charade on my sister's behalf would've never worked if Wes didn't believe I was her. Damn, on a good day this stings, but with him? It's sheer torture.

Pull yourself together.

I scrub with the fancy hand soap on the counter until my face feels raw. Under the camouflage of running water, I weep until I exhaust my ability to make tears. Not because of Wes or what happened between us, but because it was only real to me.

Despite being twins, Raelynn was always the prettier, more outgoing one, while I evolved into the artsy band nerd. I was content with my friends and music, but the more I experimented with being more extroverted or pretty, the more I'd get mistaken for her.

It's been like that forever, but it never hurt so much as it does right now. It's excruciating to accept the fact that during my happiest moments, I feel like an imposter. And when I made love with Wes, I really *was* an imposter.

Get dressed.

I groan as I tuck my girls into the corset and pull the laces from behind. It doesn't fit like it does when someone helps, but with the topcoat and Wes's leather jacket, I should make it out of here without attracting too much attention, all things considered.

Text Huey.

By the time I've dressed and put my mask back on, Huey texts me to let know he's outside. I ask him to tell Greg he can leave. I don't want to deal with him or argue about where I'm supposed to be.

I'm done.

When Huey sees me wrapped in Wes's long coat, a look of realization crosses his face but disappears fast.

"Are you ready to go?" Huey asks after clearing his throat.

"Yes. Straight home," I reply while walking toward the exit.

Wordlessly, Huey leads me down the back stairs of the

VIP lounge. When we reach the main floor, I can hear the band playing and Wes's haunting, powerful voice. For a moment I stop to listen, as it becomes a struggle to decide if hearing him sing makes me feel better or worse.

From the back stairs, I have a birds-eye view of the stage. Wes stands in the center, wearing nothing but leather pants. As he sings, his voice casts a spell on the audience, especially the women crowding the edge of the stage who reach out and try to touch him. When he leans over and brushes his fingers against their outstretched hands, they gasp, giggle, and announce the obvious to everyone.

Yeah. I've had enough.

"Are you okay, Rose?" Huey asks.

"Fine. Let's go."

Huey's hand clasps me under the elbow and whisks me out the back door.

Things will be better tomorrow. And in few days, we'll all forget about it.

CHAPTER NINE

ROSE

"There's a picture of Wes Anders kissing your ass trending on Instagram." Raelynn's words hit with the force of a sledgehammer over the phone.

My body jolts into a sitting position on the chaise lounge beside the pool, and I wince at the merciless pounding of my temples. Since the night of the launch, I've been trying to avoid Raelynn. At first it wasn't hard. She spent the rest of the weekend at Sergio's. By the time she got home early Monday afternoon, I'd left already.

For the last few days, I've escaped to the backyard pool under the pretense of a morning swim. The truth is, I lay here sipping an ice-cold latte in super-slow motion, hoping to avoid my sister, and if that's not possible, I beeline to the shower.

But since she is my employer, we live in the same house, and I'm never without my cellphone, I'm easy to find. Damn it.

"I've haven't checked the feed today." The businesslike crispness of my tone is impressive.

"Do a search for #bootycallz. Like you'd have trouble finding it."

"Is there a problem?"

"The angle is far from flattering, but at least his profile blocks out most of your ass."

"Well, Rae, if it bothers you that much, maybe you should try showing up for your own gig next time. Then you can be sure everything is all about you, just the way you like it," I snap.

"I take it you had a nice time at the party?" she says after a long pause.

"Depends on you who ask."

"I'm asking you, Rosalie."

"Why didn't tell you me that Wes Anders has a massive, MASSIVE hard-on for you?"

"What?" Raelynn's gasp is audible over the phone.

"Don't even try," I say. "He gave me an earful about it when we were alone. How could you send me there and not tell me?" My voice is filled with hurt and anger.

"Shit. I don't believe it." Raelynn moans in frustration. "He flirts, sure. That happens all the time. But it doesn't mean there was anything to it."

"What do the two of you talk about?" I demand to know.

"Mostly I try to avoid telling him what an epic bore I think he is."

"What?"

"Rose, I've said it from day one. Wes Anders does nothing for me. If he finds me interesting it's because of our discussions about music during long, awkward waits in limousines and on red carpets."

"Music? You don't know anything about music. What on earth did you say?"

"Mostly I repeated things you said after you learned I'd met him."

"Rae!" A flush creeps over my face. "You told him those things? That was a private conversation."

"You never said that," she huffs. "I needed something to talk about before I lost my damn mind. Besides, music is one of a narrow range of topics I trust your opinion on."

"Gee, thanks."

"I didn't mean it like that. And I didn't call to argue."

"Then why did you?" I ask, already knowing the answer. She wants me to do something above and beyond what my job description covers.

"The night of the gala, Wes texted me like a madman. He was worried something was wrong… do you know anything about that?"

Oh Shit.

At the launch party, Huey insisted I leave the GPS tracker active on my phone while I was in the club. It was dead by the time I left HotZone, which means Wes's texts went to straight to Raelynn.

"Really? Wh-a, what did he want?"

"For the most part he just kept apologizing over and over. Then he asked if I was okay. What's that about?"

"He wanted me to come watch his set and I bailed.

Like I warned you, that big party scene is your thing, not mine."

"That's fine. From what I've seen and heard, the launch was a success. There are plenty of pictures and buzz on social, so he's got no room to complain."

"Then everything's good, right?"

"Not exactly. Apparently, bailing on his set really put him off and he wants to come to the house and discuss it with me."

"Where are you?" I ask.

"In the car, driving. I have meetings all day and then I'm heading back to Sergio's this afternoon."

My twin radar goes straight to red-alert, and without her saying another word I grasp what she wants.

"Hell, no. I will never ever, pretend to be you again. N-E-V-E-R ever. Got it?" It's rare for me to lose my temper with her. I'm the calm, collected sister. She's the precocious, mercurial artist. "Sort your issues out with Sergio and your PR arrangement with Wes Anders. But count me out."

"You don't have to impersonate me. Just be yourself. But please take care of this for me."

"Why can't you do it?"

"Because Sergio's never believed my relationship with Wes is fake, and if I go cancelling plans with him at the last minute to meet Wes, it will be a disaster." I hear the fear and dread in her voice. "Rose, I really like Sergio. A lot. Help me out, okay?"

I don't know what comes first, the tears running down my cheeks or the cold sweat on the back of my neck. I know the reason Wes is worried and why he wants to talk.

Until I figure out how to handle this disastrous situation, it's probably not a good idea for them meet alone.

"When?" I ask.

"Late afternoon," she gulps. "I think he wants to talk and then offer to take me to dinner."

"I'm meeting Nicole tonight."

"Listen, your next night out with your BFF is on me if you do this. Please, Rose?"

"I'll take care of it," I answer.

CHAPTER TEN

WES

"*You should go,*" *she'd insisted.*

Angel Eyes had made herself clear, and it tore me into pieces. A piece that wanted to stay with her, another desperate to give in to her wishes, and a third that needed to leave.

With the success of *Jester's Edge* at stake, I couldn't stay.

Music, especially my own, has always been an outlet for me whenever I've felt trapped. Emotion, circumstance, helplessness, all these things draw me back to it, time and time again. Our encounter at HotZone created the perfect storm churning in the pit of my stomach.

I knew, *knew* it was a huge mistake to leave her naked and crying on the couch after our frenzied encounter.

Running out of there half dressed no doubt made her feel used and discarded. Of all the women I've been with or could have, she is the last one I'd want to feel mistreated by me.

My body was still slick with sweat and sex, so getting my mesh shirt back on was impossible, and I ended up playing barefoot. Lucky for me the fans went wild for my half-dressed performance.

It hurt like hell when Greg told me she left with her security ten minutes after we started.

What the hell? No goodbye? Not even a text?

That's when I knew I'd really fucked up.

Panicked and frustrated, I called her phone, but it kept going to voicemail. After my third message, she texted back.

RAE: Kinda busy.
ME: WTF?!? Are you okay?
RAE: Um… yeah.
ME: I'm so sorry about tonight.
{{Long pause}}
RAE: Don't worry about it.
ME: How can I not worry? Wish things turned out different.
RAE: Can we talk another time? I can't do this right now.
ME: I'll visit you this week. Thinking of you…

The dark green security SUV drives by a second time since I parked in front of Raelynn Tailor's house. The uniformed guard glares through his open passenger window when he passes, leaving me to wonder if he recognizes me and thinks *Jester's Edge* sucks or he's assessing the possibility that I'm a stalker.

This shouldn't surprise me. She lives in a well-established, upscale community just north of Ventura Boulevard. The house is an old Spanish revival that dates back to the nineteen thirties. Like many properties in the area, it's kind of famous, having appeared in several major feature films made during the Golden Age.

Despite the notoriety of the neighborhood, people here value their privacy.

When the guard drives away this time, he's speaking into a radio while watching my car from the rear-view mirror. It's clear that if I'm here when he returns, there'll be some bullshit to shovel. If he sees the fifteen-hundred dollar I-fucked-up-big time-bouquet on my passenger seat, that might add to the pile.

When the SUV turns the corner, I muster the courage to hop out of my 1970 Chevy Chevelle convertible and haul the massive flower arrangement up the long walkway that leads up to the front porch.

Since I didn't know what kind of flowers she liked, I asked for all of them. The bouquet includes hundreds of individual flowers. Roses, lilies, tulips, dahlias, and orchids, plus a few types I hadn't ever heard of until the florist suggested them.

Maybe it's a bit of overkill, but I know from experience that when it comes to impressing women, size matters. The size of the of bouquet, the size of the ring, the size of the bank account, and last but not least, cock size. I'm feeling pretty good about all my sizes when the front door opens.

"Can I help you?"

Wowz.

A sexy brunette with oversized horn-rimmed glasses stands in the narrow space between the open door and the jamb. Her prim, crisp, fitted white blouse is tucked into the belted waist of a tight, hounds tooth pencil skirt that falls just above her knee. Endless pin-up legs are killing it in red high-heeled pumps.

But it's her face that startles me the most.

The mesmerizing combination of perfect symmetry, golden skin, dark lashes, and the bright blue eyes are both stunning and familiar. As I stare, stunned and speechless, she watches me with an expectant expression while her weight shifts to her back hip.

"Uh, Raelynn?" It's not the right name, but the only one that comes to mind.

"She's not here," the gorgeous brunette replies. "Can I help you with something?"

"I'm supposed to meet Raelynn today. Do you know when she'll be home?"

"No idea," she says. "Sorry."

"So am I." It's worse than I thought. "These are for her."

Her gorgeous face softens as I hold up the gigantic bouquet.

"Wow. Those are beautiful," she tells me.

I give her my best panty-melting smile. "I can bring them inside if you want."

She bites her petal-pink lip in a gesture that's both sexy as hell and hauntingly familiar.

"Sure." She gestures with a graceful twist of her wrist. "Come in."

Squeezing between her and the door brings me close to the glossy waves of her walnut brown hair. As I inhale, the subtle scents of vanilla, lavender, and mint overwhelm me with intimate memories that are out of place. It takes all of my willpower to not move closer and run my fingers through the dark brown strands.

She looks up at me with a strange, questioning expression before she lowers her eyes.

Get a fucking grip, Wes.

"Um," she clears her throat. "Why don't you set them there." She points to a wide round table centered in the large foyer. "They'll be the first thing Raelynn sees when she comes home."

As I lay them on the ornate hardwood table with inlaid marble, she retrieves a huge vase from a nearby closet. Its ready accessibility tells me this house receives a lot of flower deliveries.

There's a peaceful silence as she transfers the gigantic bouquet into the large, ice-blue vase.

"Cymbidium orchids?" She notes with a smile. "How thoughtful."

"You like them?" I'm pleased at the possibility.

Her expression saddens. It distresses me. "Well, they're not for me, so I suppose it doesn't matter."

"I really hope Raelynn likes them," I tell her.

The stunner pauses a moment, schooling her remarks with practiced care. "She'll appreciate the gesture. But that will be as far as it goes." She nods with a sad smile.

"You... know what happened?" My throat is dry. "She told you about it?"

Who is this woman?

"Not in so many words. But the two-thousand dollar please-forgive-me bouquet from *Billet-doux* fills in the blanks."

Speechless, I wipe my sweaty palms along the thighs of my jeans and watch as she wordlessly goes about her task.

"Can I help?" I ask after a few moments of silence.

"You enjoy flower arrangements?" she asks

"Sort of." It's half true. "There's an obvious skill to it. As a musician, the transformation of ordinary elements into something extraordinary interests me a great deal."

She laughs and gestures for me to join her at the table.

"I'm Wes."

"Yes, I remember," she replies.

"You... remember? Have we met?" From the minute she answered the door, I've felt a crazy mix of attraction, tension, and confusion.

"We did. Here," she waves around the entryway. "The night of the Musician of the Year Awards."

"Are you sure?" I shake my head.

A look of disappointed resignation crosses her face. "I sewed a button back on your shirt when you came to pick up Raelynn." Plum colored fingernails reach toward my throat but stop before they touch me.

It feels like someone tattooed a well-deserved 'A' for

asshole across my forehead in big, bold, bleeding red letters.

"I remember that night… and the button. That was you?" I'm skeptical.

"Afraid so."

"Thank you." I hesitate. "I'm sorry I didn't recognize you. It was a completely crazy evening for me."

"It was a stressful evening," she admits.

"Yes." My eyes will her to look at me, and when she does, I continue. "You also seem really different today."

"Different?" Her chin juts out, like she's waiting to be insulted. "How?"

"Well, for starters you were wearing a pin cushion in your hair."

She remains silent, but her weight shifts backward again. Clearly, she didn't expect me to remember that.

"I must've looked ridiculous."

"Not to me. I'd just lost a button on my two-thousand-dollar shirt ahead of a live television appearance. At that moment you were my guardian angel."

She says nothing. Instead, her focus turns to the bouquet as she fans the individual flowers out and arranges the ones at the edges so they're not being crushed.

"Beautiful." The word is out of my mouth before I can stop myself, and I don't know whether I'm talking about the flower arrangement or her.

"Thank you," she replies without looking at me.

"You never told me your name that night."

"You never asked." She quietly folds the tissue paper

that surrounded the flowers and places it back into
the box.

She's right. Raelynn had joined us and I'd lost sight of
everything else.

"Can I ask now?"

"Rosalie," she shrugs. "Rosalie Tailor."

Jesus H. Christ.

"Tailor? *Tailor?* You two are sisters?"

She looks at me like I'm the biggest dumb fuck on the
planet. "You didn't notice the resemblance?"

"Of course I did, that's why I've been distracted since
you opened the door. You look just like her, but you're
different in so many ways."

Rosalie rolls her eyes, and it's clear my observations
aren't taken as compliments. "Maybe she looks like me."

"Excuse me?"

"We're twins!"

"Twins," I repeat in a daze.

The news should surprise, even amuse me. Instead, I
break out in a cold sweat.

After months of work conflicts and communication
fuck-ups, Raelynn Tailor showed up at my launch party
dressed like a goddess from an X-rated funhouse. Whenever I close my eyes, our satisfied groans drive me to
distraction.

Now, when I open them, her sister stands in front
of me.

"You're so different. The night of the award ceremony
you radiated calm and competence in a sea of chaos."

"That's very kind of you," she shrugs.

"Do you live here too?"

"Yes." She looks straight at me. "It's a perk and a drawback of the job. Room and board are included, but I'm accessible twenty-four seven."

"Sounds good to me," I reply.

What I meant to say and how it sounded changes the atmosphere between us.

Rosalie's eyes drop, and she folds her hands together. I follow her gaze, then survey those toned thighs, trim waist, and pert breasts. When I look up, those full lips are parted as she watches me watch her.

This is wrong, I warn myself.

"It was nice meeting you again, Rosalie." I remove my phone from the back pocket of my jeans to check the time. "Please tell Raelynn I stopped by."

"Of course," she replies. "Let me show you out."

We walk toward the door together. The only sound is the click-click of Rosalie's heels on the marble floor. When we both reach for the handle at the same time, my hand ends up grasping hers. The flesh and feel of her palm and fingers are warm and alive. The smell or her hair and the familiar curves all pose a potent temptation for me.

They're twins, I remind myself over and over.

"Goodbye, Rose."

A sad, disappointed expression mars her beautiful features. "Goodbye."

CHAPTER ELEVEN

ROSE

"*H*i!" I wave and knock on the large picture window of *Lola's Place*.

Nicole looks up from her phone and waves back before I leave for the main entrance.

It's Friday after a week from hell and I can't wait to decompress over drinks with my BFF. Nicole and I go all the way back to high school in San Diego. Our relationship waned a little after she moved to Los Angeles for university, while I stayed closer to home. We got back in touch when I relocated here to work after graduation, and we became close friends again.

"Wow… guess you win the prize for most bizarre week," she greets me. "First round's on me."

As Nicole handles our drink orders, I glance down at

our recent text exchanges. I've been texting Nikki about my dilemma and now, rereading our exchanges, it hits me how crazy my life must seem to others. When our server leaves, I shut my cell phone off and look at Nikki.

She gives me an incredulous shake of her head and a smile that's full of recrimination.

"I know…" I speak before she can.

"So… you attended a launch party for…" she looks around the room and lowers her voice. We both know to be careful not to mention names. "… where you hooked up with *him*. But you went there pretending to be your sister and now *he* thinks he slept with *her?*"

"Yeah." I gulp.

"Well, you always did have it bad for the boys in the band," Nikki tells me after a few moments.

"I'm not a groupie."

"Never said that. As I recall, it was more a birds-of-a-feather kind of thing." She takes a sip from her glass. "But you've never been one for a hit-and-run… what's up with that?"

"I've… liked him for a while. He has a mad, mad, crush on my sister, and when he came on to me—"

"—because he thought you were her,"

"Yeah. That's right." I agree.

She stares at me a few moments, then swirls her drink and takes a large sip. "Do you still play the guitar, Rose? Write any songs lately?"

"Of course. Whenever I get the chance."

"Mmm. You mean when Raelynn doesn't have you chasing her tail."

"I *do* work for her."

"For how long now?" she asks. "It was never clear to me how soon after you moved in that you became her assistant."

I bristle at the question, but it's only fair to answer, because it's a discussion I've always avoided. It's not a secret, more like a crappy time in my life that I don't like to discuss.

"The Christmas they cancelled my television series."

"The position you landed while you were still in college?"

"Yeah. I couldn't move here fast enough after graduation. Then they canceled my show the following season. After that, I strung together a few gigs writing scores and jingles for commercials. But I still couldn't make rent, and couch surfing started to suck. In fact, it pissed Raelynn off when she found out about it."

"That's when you moved in with her?"

"She insisted," I remember. "Rae had just bought her house."

Raelynn had begun modeling in high school, then went up to LA for college but never attended. She's been with the same San Diego agents since her mid-teens, and they were well connected here. A few right moves, some lucky breaks, the ceaseless drive to work grueling hours, and voila! Supermodel success.

"Is that when you became her assistant?"

"She had just done a major swimsuit shoot." I nod at the memory. "Overbooked, overworked, with a lot of money coming and going and no one she trusted to look after it."

"And there you were, down on your luck, feeling guilty, looking for ways to help," Nicole offers.

"I wanted to be a good guest, a good sister." It's an easy, truthful admission.

"Now I know how she keeps you around and talks you into this shit."

"What are you talking about?"

"I've been watching your sister act for a long time now, Rose. And the thing I notice is that Raelynn gets what she wants, while you're constantly waiting your turn."

Nicole's not wrong, she's my BFF, and she's often clashed with my sister because of it. In fact, Nikki's one of the few people who can still tell Raelynn off, a skill that makes me eternally envious. Nikki's never forgotten how difficult it is for me to have my closest friend and twin sister at each other's throats, while Raelynn has been less sympathetic.

"It's complicated," I insist. "We're twins. The line's never stopped being blurred. And it only gets worse the more successful she gets."

"What about you? Don't you want your own career? Or do you plan on giving it up to be Raelynn's assistant?"

I blow out a slow breath and lace my fingers across my forehead. "Every time I bring up the subject of quitting, she panics. It's never a good time." My own words fill me with despair. "Her business and brands have grown so much *I* need an assistant."

"Oh, Rose." Nicole shakes her head at me. "If you leave it up to her, the answer will be no forever. I've always tried to bite my tongue when your sister comes up, for your sake, not hers, but she's someone who sucks all the oxygen out of a room and is way too self-absorbed to notice people close to her suffocating."

When I glare at Nikki, she throws her hands into the air. "I'm sorry if I hurt you, but I don't regret what I said."

I'm angry. Not because of what she said, but because it's the truth. And part of me has known it for a long time.

"You're right, Nikki. It's just that… sometimes giving in is a hell of a lot easier than fighting about things with her. Other times, I still feel like I owe her."

"Cut the cord, my friend. Let it all go. Start looking for work as a composer. Are you in touch with anyone from your old show? How about from university? Find a job and quit working for Raelynn. It's the only way."

"And what about this… situation between Rae and Wes?"

"He brought her flowers and she didn't call him?"

I shake my head.

She laughs. "Well, that's that then. He's got way too much ego, and good reason for it, to put up with that kind of treatment. It's done."

"You're probably right." Although the realization makes me uneasy.

"I know." She signals the server as she approaches our table. "Another round, Rose?"

"Sure."

CHAPTER TWELVE

WES

"*W*hat's the deal with Raelynn Tailor?" Jai asks, tuning his bass.

"It's not looking good, guys." I mean it in multiple ways.

Almost two weeks since the launch party and we've had no contact. Zero. Zilch. Nada. I've called, left messages, no response. When I texted, her sister Rosalie responded at once, and explained that she'd now answer all my calls and texts to her sister.

Raelynn fucking ghosted me. Shit.

The timing of our hookup sucked. But Christ, why am I the bad guy? She came on to me and enjoyed it every bit as much as I did. That alone should be worth a second chance, or at least a returned call.

"Is she still doing our video?" Vince asks from his seat behind his drums.

I stare out at killer views of the city skyline from the lower level of my secluded hillside home in Los Feliz. The sliding oak-framed glass doors open out to a zero-edge pool and a pleasant breeze skips along the water and into the house where me and my bandmates talk and rehearse.

Another perfect day in sunny southern California.

But today it does nothing for me because the Raelynn Tailor dilemma is turning into a major mine field of mind-fucks, and the entire mess is biting me in the ass.

It's Sunday afternoon and the guys are at my house on the pretext of going over some song arrangements, but they're really here to hash some things out. I brace myself for blowback as I answer Vince's question.

"I doubt it."

Prior to our launch party, the band's management team was negotiating her role in our latest music video. The arrangement was separate from our PR contract, and it was a done deal except for the finalized agreement. Or so we believed until yesterday when her agent informed ours that she couldn't take part due to scheduling conflicts.

"How you'd mess that up, Wes? You seemed to get along well enough at the party," he barks from behind his drum set.

At thirty-four, he's our oldest member.

Before he joined Jester's Edge, Vince had been a drummer for two highly respected but marginally successful bands. When I had approached him, he was a real diva but didn't have many choices. His last band had broken up again, and he'd grown tired of the whiplash and not getting paid.

He's always been amped up about everything. Music, money, women. Especially women. He's been seething since the whole supermodel-rocker PR arrangement started. Vince isn't jealous, he just owns a warped competitive streak. It like he's running a race and his only hope of winning is if the guy in front trips and falls.

We go head-to-head a lot. But eight years and forty million sale units under our belt make me comfortable telling him to shove it whenever the need arises.

"She is a famous supermodel," Jai chimes in as he plays a simple chord progression on his bass. "Why is it so hard to understand that her schedule's overbooked? Relax, Vince. Not everything is a calculated attempt to piss you off."

Jai had been straight out of high school when he joined my band. He'd looked about twelve when we met, but damn, could he grind an axe and seduce a keyboard. He's always been the band's peacemaker.

"Well, Darius Lefebre gets busy too." No one was happier than Vince when the world-famous video director signed on to our project.

"Darius Lefebre is on you," I say. "You insisted we move heaven and earth to accommodate him. The pre-production schedule was already a nightmare. Raelynn Tailor books out months in advance. This isn't her fault. It's mine."

"Yours?" They repeat in unison.

In more ways than one. "I shouldn't have agreed to delay production to suit Darius. Now, because I didn't want to be a dicK-tator, we've got no female lead. If we revise the schedule again, we'll probably lose our director too."

"What do we do about Dirty Little Liar?" Jai asks in his ever-calm voice. "Should we hire someone else?"

I respond with a few chords of a new melody that's haunted me awhile. Jai and Vince listen as I reach the point where the melody becomes obscure. Despite our differences on the inside, we're all true musicians and sometimes we use music to speak to each other. They don't rush me because they understand from the angst in my playing that I'm working on both an answer and a song.

"We can find another actor or model, sure. But the thing is, we've been building up this PR push with Raelynn Tailor for months now. If we hire anyone else, those efforts go down the drain."

"Someone needs to sit on Raelynn Tailor's scheduler." Vince punctuates his words with a drum roll and ends with a forceful strike of his cymbal.

"What did you say?" I look up from my guitar and quit playing.

"All the back-and-forth BS has to quit." His drums rumble as he beats them with an escalating edge of excitement. "We need to figure out when she's free, go through a few rounds of give and take and get this done."

"Rose." Her name springs from my mouth with such relief I half-sing it.

"Who's that?" Jai asks.

"Raelynn Tailor's sister. She's also her PA."

"Do you know her?" Jai asks.

"A little. Yeah." I realize now that the guys haven't met Rose because she wasn't with Rae at our launch. The driver and security guard came, but no one else, which is strange.

"Can she help us with this scheduling nightmare?" Vince asks.

Good question.

I've fucked up with both the Tailor sisters. When I went to Raelynn's house and found a diplomatic and defensive Rose, I didn't remember our earlier meeting.

In my defense, she'd transformed from that encounter.

It never dawned on me that the super-confident, hyper-efficient, sexy nerd who accepted the flowers I brought to Raelynn was the same woman I'd met months ago.

If they've confided in each other about me, there's a good chance they agree I'm some special brand of asshole.

"She might be able to do a lot more than that," I reply.

They are twins. Identical twins. Rosalie could easily do pre-production and some actual production work. That should bring the time Raelynn needs to present down to a minimum. With Rose's help, it's possible we can get this damn video made with the director and model we wanted all along.

"I'm going to make a few calls. I'll let you guys know what happens."

CHAPTER THIRTEEN

ROSE

"This is good for you. You should agree to this deal," I tell her from the kitchen counter while pouring myself coffee with a splash of whole milk.

"The hell it is," Raelynn grumbles from the breakfast nook as she crinkles then tosses a familiar document with bullet points and highlights away in disgust.

I take my time slowly cleaning up in the kitchen. It's best to let her rant a bit. Unlike ordinary mornings, where we might offer to bring each other something, I remain silent until I sit down beside her.

She takes the agreement back, gasps in disgust, then tosses it in my direction. I pick it up and pretend to read it for a few minutes before I speak.

"In order to get what you want, you've got to give

Wes Anders what he needs. There's no other way to resolve this," I inform my sister. "Besides, it's a near perfect solution."

"Easy for you to say," Raelynn pouts.

"Oh, please," I remind her. "They're using me as your body double. I do the fittings and most of the scenes. You've got a day's work, maybe another half, tops. Besides that, Wes has agreed to cancel your personal appearances contract."

After I told Rae about Wes's mad crush on her, she's been even more eager to bail on their collaboration. Sergio being resentful of the façade Raelynn's career requires her to keep up was one thing, but dealing with the flirtatious advances of an edgy, sexy rock star put it over the line.

Raelynn remains silent as she stands and walks into the kitchen, takes out the ingredients for her protein smoothie, and fires up the blender. The whirring noise bothers me this early in the morning, so I move to the kitchen table by the French doors that overlook the backyard.

Raelynn's house is tranquil, but living here with her... well, that's another matter. Maybe it wouldn't be so bad if I didn't work for her? I'm not sure. Until this agreement with Wes ends, living with her will only be more difficult. I don't want to be a buffer anymore, especially with him.

It was wrong to attend the launch impersonating my sister. I've always hated switching, and not because she benefits the most. She asks me, I don't ask her. Now, every attempt I make to become successful and independent creates comparisons and cases of mistaken identity.

As for Wes... I owe him.

Although hearing him scream out my sister's name during sex was more than ample punishment, it's only led to bigger problems. If he'd known it was me who'd answered his texts, kissed him like a boss, and traded orgasms with him, life would be different now. Very different.

Those sexed-up pictures wouldn't exist, let alone be trending on social media. Sergio wouldn't be angry and jealous. Wes and Raelynn would've hammered out an agreement for his Pretty Little Liar video.

Yeah, I owe. And payback's a bitch.

The whirring of the blender stops, and I look out the window while Raelynn screws the lid onto her metallic smoothie cup and inserts a reusable bamboo straw. From the corner of my eye, I watch her size me up, calculating how much of a hard time I'm prepared to give her. I force myself to relax while I stare out at the well-manicured yard and pool while sipping my morning java in peace.

Raelynn walks toward the French doors, but as she's about to go outside, she takes a seat next to me like it's an afterthought.

"How's Sergio?" I prod gently.

"This contract stuff with Wes makes it hard."

I nod and take a casual sip of my coffee. "Sergio does understand you're a model, right? And that personal appearances are your bread and butter? You want out of your contract, fine. There are other options, for now at least. But never forget that those engagements with Wes boosted sales of your brands too. They make you real money."

Raelynn twists an end of long blonde hair with her index finger and pulls it tight.

"Modeling isn't the problem," she sighs, and wraps her hands around the smoothie cup. "It's friends and acquaintances who see pictures of Wes and I as a couple. It's difficult to explain because of the contract, so Sergio ends up looking daft and whipped. He's not happy about it. Neither am I."

"You know Wes can sue you for breach, right? At the very least he's entitled to compensation."

"Maybe I should just pay him," she muses.

"You can't, Rae. I've been through this with your agent."

"Why the hell not?"

"Because your breach will cost them more than the price of your time. He could come after you for revenue losses, which are easy to show, given your established working relationship. Everyone made money from this, Raelynn, even you. That's why the suits did the happy dance over this contract."

She blows out a tired breath. "You're the last person I thought who'd be on board with this."

"Why?"

"Because you hate it when my life takes over yours."

"Thanks for noticing." I shrug. "How is this any different?"

"You don't enjoy modeling, you never have. And you loathe impersonating me," Raelynn nods slowly. "I should be talking you into this, not the other way around."

My legs shift uncomfortably under the table.

"My first choice is that you meet all your contractual obligations. You made a commitment and it's financially lucrative. It's also time for you to face the fact that Wes isn't the problem. It's you and Sergio. But… until you part ways with Wes, being around you is going to suck. The music video allows me to pick my poison and decide when to stop drinking."

"Fine." Raelynn's shoulders droop and she stares at the wood grain of the kitchen table as she traces the grooves with a long, manicured fingernail. "I'll agree to do it in exchange for termination of the personal appearances contract. But who's going to do your job while you're on set?"

"I've spoken to Nicole."

"Nicole?" Rae's eyes widen. "Seriously?"

"Yeah. We've both known her since high school, and aside from being my BFF, she's trustworthy. Besides, school's out for the summer and she could use the extra cash."

Nicole works as a student school counselor in the public school system. Her typical summer is a mix of odd jobs and travel. If she can handle SoCal teens for a living, she should be able to survive our three-ring circus.

"Of course, she'll need to be paid," I remind her.

Rae gives a shrug of resignation. "When does all this start?"

"ASAP after you agree to terms. Probably a few weeks out."

"Fine." She stands with her coffee cup but leaves the wrinkled document behind. "Should I call my agent or can you handle that?"

"I'll take care of it. Let's get this done, okay?"

"Sure."

Without another word, Rae opens the French doors and heads outside.

CHAPTER FOURTEEN

ROSE

"*I* don't understand how you could ever agree to this," Nicole tells me from the passenger seat.

"It's not obvious, but it does make sense," I insist, focusing on the road as we exit the highway.

"It makes no sense," she insists. "You never liked to model. You hate impersonating your sister, and now you've jumped in with both feet for Wes Anders."

"What's wrong with Wes Anders?" I glance over at Nicole, who rolls her eyes and responds with a doubtful glare.

"One, you had sex with him. While he thought you were Raelynn. An incident in your saner moments you believe needs to be buried behind the shed. Now, he's paying you to pretend to be her in a video? Do you not see the deranged contradictions?"

"Wes doesn't know the truth about that night." I try hard to keep the sadness from my voice. "There's no deranged motivation on his part."

"And what about you?"

"I can't unravel my professional life from hers until we fulfill her obligations to Wes. The longer it takes, the longer I'm in limbo. Video production will be over in a week instead of months. I'll suck it up. It's nothing I haven't done before."

"And that's why you're doing this?" she asks. "Because you want to quit working for Rae?"

"I also want to follow your advice." I shoot her a quick smile. "You told me to get a job in the music business, remember?"

"Your job on this video doesn't involve music!"

"It's a step in the right direction."

Nicole folds her arms and stares out the window as the GPS lets us know that we've arrived. My pearl-colored Prius crawls down a long driveway before stopping at the kiosk near the entrance to the sound stage Jester's Edge rented for their video production. It's one of the larger independent studios popular for music videos.

"How's it going?" I call out to the security guard through the driver's side window.

"Not bad for a Monday. First day?" he asks.

"First time," I answer.

"Need to see your pass, please."

As I start to rummage through the console, Nicole

hands me the fed ex envelope and we exchange heartfelt smiles.

"Fifty-four-A… go left, left, right, then left. Keep this on your mirror." He returns my pass.

We drive off in silence as I concentrate on finding the studio entrance. After we park and I turn the car off, Nicole and I sit quietly for a few moments.

"Thank you for helping me through this, Nikki. I really appreciate it." I give her forearm a gentle pat.

"You are my best friend from like… forever. I have your back, okay? But please… be careful. I've known you both a long time, and Raelynn has always been the dominant, bossy twin. I love your parents, but life as a school counselor tells me they should've done more to curb her Queen Bee syndrome, at least where you were concerned."

"Me too. But I can't change her, Nikki. The only thing I can do is learn to take care of myself better."

"That's my point, Rose. And that's why I'm worried about you and Wes Anders. It's like you've gone and replaced one high maintenance diva with another. One you're crushing on madly."

"I don't anymore. Not really." Suddenly the desire to talk leaves me and I reach behind the seat to grab my purse.

"You're not one for casual hook-ups. Never have been never will be."

"I know, but I can stay focused when it comes to Wes. There's no way we could be together without him knowing the truth, and I can't tell him." My head shakes and sadness overwhelms me. "That's assuming he'd even be interested, which I doubt. The humiliation is too much."

Nikki sighs and clasps my hand. "You sure you're up for this?" she asks.

"I'm positive," I reply with more confidence than I feel.

CHAPTER FIFTEEN

WES

The elephant doors next to the soundstage entrance creak open seconds before a medium-sized delivery truck backs into the cargo bay.

I arrived before seven this morning, but the last vehicle carrying set props was delayed because of a highway accident. Our pre-production meeting starts in ten minutes, and Vince hasn't arrived yet.

This is the first video I've taken a producer's role on, and it's off to a rough start. Hell, just getting the female lead to show up has been a fucking nightmare.

Thank God for Rosalie Tailor.

The truth is, I didn't have high hopes after speaking with Rose on the phone.

"I need your help, Rose."

"Me? For what?"

"You know about our Pretty Little Liar video?"

"The one you can't get made because you hired Darius the diva to direct?"

"Isn't that a little harsh?"

"Not at all. My sister and I have both worked with Darius before."

"Raelynn's worked with Darius before?"

"Yeah, and good luck with that."

I pressed the phone against my chest, cursed a few times, then blurted out my idea.

"I want to hire you to work on our video as your sister's body double. It'll reduce her time commitment and make it work with her schedule... will you do it?"

"Me? I think you've got the wrong Tailor sister."

"Well, she won't talk to me, so you're my last hope."

I pleaded and coaxed for almost an hour. She promised to try her best, but when she hung up and left me alone with the ruthless silence of dead air, I assumed it was dead on arrival.

But then a miracle took place.

Within in days, the Tailor sisters were both on board. They wanted to cancel the PR contract, but I'd already agreed to that when Raelynn slept with me for the first and last time.

Truth to tell, I feel a strange mix of gleeful, grateful, and guilty. It's amazing that Darius Lefebre and Raelynn Tailor will both be part of the video for this song.

I'm indebted to Rosalie for all the wheeling and dealing she did with Rae's agency and Darius' studio to make this work, not to mention the persuasive tactics she used on her sister. This wouldn't have worked out without her. I've never been so dependent on someone with so little invested in the outcome.

My outcome. It fills me with a sense of uneasy vulnerability that keeps me on edge.

"The big day's here." Jai comes up beside me to watch the truck unload.

"About damn time," I grumble.

"Are you up for this?" he asks.

"Think so. Hope so. We'll see, I guess."

"I have faith in you. I always did. That's why I agreed to join your band," Jai tells me.

"Thanks. It's been one helluva ride, and we're fucking lucky." I look around the cargo bay. "Speaking of luck, have you seen Vince today?"

"No. You think he'll show?"

"Of course he will. Eventually. Vince just likes to be a pain in my ass."

Jai blows out a breath and sighs. "I'll call him and make sure he's on his way."

"Thanks. Before this is over, me and Vince are bound to cross swords a few more times. I need to choose my battles."

"I know."

Jai removes his phone from the front pocket of his jeans. When he looks up at the parking lot, he stops and does a double take.

"Hell-O. Who's that?" he asks.

As I step outside the open doors, it's easy to see who Jai is talking about. The attractive woman removing items from the trunk of a white Prius catches my eye too.

Tall, toned, and dark-haired, her oval shaped faced is obscured by sunglasses. High-heeled wedge sandals wrap up just beneath her calves, flattering the athletic legs underneath her cropped jeans. A frilly, mauve-colored vest tied into a knot exposes her flat stomach and slender waist above the low-cut light denim.

"Rosalie?" I say out loud, stunned.

"You know her?"

"Um, yeah." She looks so… different.

Whenever I see Rose, she's undergone a dramatic transformation from our previous encounter. Today, any resemblance to the no-nonsense, hyper-prim assistant that greeted me a month ago doesn't exist.

Her clothes are casual and flattering, making it easy to notice an obvious weight loss since our last meet up. No doubt she felt pressed to slim down for this video shoot. A pang of guilt and disappointment overtake me. I liked her fuller, softer figure.

"Please tell me we'll be working together," Jai says.

"That's Raelynn Tailor's sister," I answer in a quiet voice.

"Sister? Sweet! Do you know if she's single?"

My only response is a displeased glare intended to deter Jai's enthusiasm. It doesn't work. Not. At. All.

"Never mind." Jai clears his throat. "I'll figure it out."

"Thought you were going to call Vince?"

He gives me a dismissive wave before taking out his phone and walking off. Knowing Jai, he'll find a super casual excuse to meet Rose. His style with women is quiet, brooding, and a little intense when he's hooked. It's a far cry from Vince whose hedonistic caveman personae appeals to far more women than anyone sane would expect.

Then there's me.

Come as you are, take me as I am. Ask me no questions I'll tell you no lies. It's an approach that's worked well for me over the years. Mostly it gets me what I want when I've wanted it without complications or too many complaints. Until recently anyway.

Jai's obvious interest in Rose leaves me pondering her single status and dating preferences. As he rushes away, I wonder if Rose would prefer his liquid brown eyes, shoulder length dreadlocks, and soulful, mixed race exotic affect to straight black hair and green eyes attached to my live and let live attitude.

I shouldn't try to guess about these things. Rose is Raelynn's twin, and she's doing me a huge favor.

Don't even think about sleeping with her.

Desperate for a distraction, I take out my phone and call Vince. Where the fuck is that guy?

"It's going to be a hectic seven days, but we're all determined to make it as smooth as possible. You've got your schedules. Everyone except Rose, Millicent, and Ainsley can leave. Thanks."

It's the end of our final pre-production session, and I'm pleased to see that everyone showed up, even Vince. Our meeting took place in an open-air atrium inside the studio building. Over the years the band has attended dozens of these meetings, but this is the first time I've been in charge, and the relieved sensation overcomes and surprises me.

Thirty-odd crew members shuffle out of the conference room, leaving only Rose, the young woman who showed up with her, and production staff. Throughout the meeting, Rose and her friend scribbled notes furiously and texted between quiet whispers. It took tremendous self-discipline for me not to fixate on her.

"Hey, Rose." I try to be casual. "Thanks for being on time this morning. It's especially helpful because you're wearing a lot of hats in this production," I add for the benefit of everyone. "For the next week, Ainsley and Millicent are the most important people you'll work with while you're here."

"Hi, I'm Ainsley. The wardrobe supervisor."

"Nice to meet you," Rose replies. "You're my first appointment today," she says without checking the schedule.

"That's right. Most of the clothes have arrived, and we can start anytime. I know you work closely with your sister. Do you have final wardrobe approval or is that someone else?"

"Coraline, Raelynn's personal stylist," Rosalie's shadow announces, before she makes notes on an iPad.

"Everyone, this is Nikki, Raelynn Tailor's assistant for this project. She'll coordinate between the production team and Raelynn's staff."

Everyone nods, and a subtle shift in the way they address questions occurs.

"Nikki, will Coraline be ready to start on time?" Ainsley asks after a quick check of her watch.

"She's got fifteen minutes. I'll give her another five and call."

"If Coraline is late, start without her," Rose insists. "Let me handle any blow back."

Her statement causes raised eyebrows among the production staff. Can she really decide that?

"Are you sure?" I ask.

"Absolutely." She gives me a direct look. "Raelynn is completely rebooked for the dates freed up as a result of my participation. There is zero wiggle room in her schedule. Our part of this project must get done on time."

Rosalie holds my gaze a moment, then turns to the production crew. "If there's a problem on Raelynn Tailor's end with the schedule, her staff, anything that could cause delays, I'd appreciate being told ASAP." She looks at me again. "Please."

"Of course," I reply. "Ainsley, why don't you and Nikki go get started. Rose, Millicent, and I still need to touch base and we're running late."

Ainsley gives me a quick nod, then encourages Nikki to follow her. Once they've left, it's just the three of us.

CHAPTER SIXTEEN

ROSE

*N*ikki and Ainsley file out, while the three of us remain behind enveloped in an awkward silence. It's a little nerve-wracking for me. Productions like this run on a brutal schedule, so impromptu chats aren't usually a good sign.

Wes clears his throat and gives me a patient smile. It makes me excited and skittish all at once, and my arms encircle my torso out of nervous habit.

"Rose, I know you've spent a lot of time on various types of sets as your sister's assistant. But do you have any acting or modeling experience of your own?"

"No." I give him an honest answer. "But you never asked, so I assumed you knew that."

"It didn't matter. Your participation was so crucial to this video we needed to take you as-is."

Thanks. "Um, okay?"

My gaze shifts between Wes and the tall, elegant woman standing next to him. She's about five-foot ten, with perfect dark mahogany skin, and silver, shoulder length cornrows. Her sleeveless collared shirt and wide olive-green pants are the epitome of stylish and professional.

She steps between us and extends her hand. "Hello, I'm Millicent. I'll be working with you on the video."

"Working with me?" With each moment, my confusion grows.

"I was a child actor who later became an acting coach," she explains patiently. "I've done consulting on many types of film and video productions."

"But I'm only doing body double work. There's no speaking role." I look at him for confirmation.

"That's right." His hands do an awkward deep-dive into his front pockets. "She's going to be your intimacy coordinator."

"Excuse me?" My *what?*

"I'll be your advocate and liaison for the intimate scenes." Her calm, assured voice only alarms me.

"That sounds like an executive role for an online dating app." I couldn't be more stunned if someone punched me in the mouth.

Raelynn does what can be described as artful and suggestive nudity. Vivid love scenes? Whenever a project calls for those, they're done by a body double with Raelynn's approval. I blow out a breath. Lucky me.

"How many are in the script?" I ask.

They exchange glances.

"There are two kissing scenes," she explains. "One is topless."

"Who are they with?" The strain in my voice is audible even to me.

"Me." Wes's stoic answer reverberates across the empty room.

"Just you?"

"Afraid so."

Cold moisture forms at the nape of my neck, and I place my hand over the slick patch. "I've never worked with an intimacy coordinator before. Why is this necessary?"

"Millicent, please give us a few minutes. You've got a meeting with Darius, and I don't want to hold you up."

"Of course." She smiles at me. "It was nice to meet you, Rose. I look forward to working with you."

"Thank you." I watch her cross the room and exit out the glass paneled double doors. When they click shut, I turn to face Wes.

"Why?" I ask.

Wes sighs, then gestures to a cluster of chairs in the center of the suite. Whatever conversation he wants to have, I'm not interested. I fold my arms and stand my ground. When he sees me resist, he picks the chair furthest from me, spins it around, and props his elbow on the backrest while he watches me.

"There's a lot at stake. I need this to go smoothly."

"And you think I'm incapable of achieving that without a coach?" I ask.

Wes's chin snaps back, his expression a mixture of frustration and distress.

"You're one of the most capable women I've ever met. This isn't about you, Rose. It's about me."

"What?" I repeat. "You've lost me."

"I fucked up with your sister. I refuse to allow the same thing to happen with you. Not here, not now."

There's something about the combination of the acoustics in this room and his almost supernatural voice that makes me shudder. He's worried about stuff he shouldn't be, but convincing him will be hard... for a lot of reasons. Including the fact that can't tell him the truth about that night.

"You're not being fair to yourself, or her, Wes." Reluctantly, I walk toward him and take the chair closest to him. "Things didn't go the way you thought they would. Life works out like that sometimes."

I know that from experience.

"Oh, but they did. That's the hell of it." His head shakes sadly. "As rushed and unexpected as our hookup was, it was the best damn night I can remember. But it ended badly. That's on me."

"No, it wasn't. Not all of it."

"I upset your sister. She obviously felt disrespected, used, and later angry. That's my fault. I had a reason to leave, a good one, but that didn't change the way I made her feel. I can't fix that, no matter what I try."

"You're wrong." I reach out and squeeze the forearm he's draped across the backrest of the chair. "She didn't think that. She was... stunned after it happened." I shake my head at the memory and share my truth. "It was so unexpected and sudden, she didn't know how to react."

"Damn it, then why won't she talk to me, or accept my apology?"

God, this is hard.

When I agreed to work on the *Wonderland Pretty Little Liar* video, I did it to make amends for the mess I'd made of Wes's plans. Commiserating with him about the demise of his 'relationship' with my sister was not something I'd read between the lines of the job description.

I should've known better. Not because of Wes or Raelynn or knowing what really happened. I've always been the go-to person when someone needs a ready box of tissues and a shoulder to cry on.

"There nothing to apologize for or talk about. The whole thing is something you should avoid," I reply.

"Why?" He explodes next to me.

"Because going through the motions of an apology and an acceptance will create unrealistic and painful expectations." My voice is soft, steady, and strong. "Raelynn has always been private about her personal life. She didn't mind pretending with you because it wasn't real, so nothing bad could happen. If it became true, she'd feel exposed. That's why she backed away."

Wes rises from the chair and paces the room. He runs his hand through his hair a few times, then squares his shoulders and adopts a resolved stance.

"It's bizarre, but in a strange way, it makes sense. Keeping anything private when your livelihood depends on feeding social media daily is next to impossible. And your sister's far more exposed than I am."

Wes's pacing ceases beside me. His dark expression bores into me, but it's like he sees nothing. The distance feels awkward, so I rise from my chair and stand close to him.

"Please don't blame Raelynn for this. It's not her fault either." His sadness upsets me.

"I don't. And I know." He speaks with resignation. "Both of us are way too successful on the marketing and PR fronts. We've sold metric tons of music, make-up, concert tickets, alcohol, and athletic clothes together. We'd never be able to stop. Our agents, labels, and brands wouldn't allow it. *We* couldn't stop it. A personal relationship would be over before it started."

"I'm so sorry. For everything, especially the fact that things didn't go the way you hoped with Raelynn." It's the truth. The more pain he feels, the more I wish it would stop.

"Dear, sweet Rose," Wes strokes my cheek with the back of his hand, "Thank you for being honest with me. You've saved me untold nights of heavy alcohol consumption."

My skin flushes at his touch, and I feel my flesh warm and turn pink. Flustered, I pull away and glance downward.

"Rose?" his deep voice demands that I look at him. When I don't, he cups my chin and forces me to look up. He studies my face, those green eyes taking their time with every detail. My whole body feels warmer, and I'm horrified that I'll be beet red in seconds.

I clasp Wes's fingers and squeeze them gently for a

moment as we stare at each other. He's about to say something, but before he can, I do.

"I should leave."

My wedge sandals make a muted, hollow sound as I hurry to the door. My heart races so loudly that it's the only noise I hear. This is going to be much harder than even I imagined.

CHAPTER SEVENTEEN

ROSE

"*O*w! Damn it, Ainsley." I hiss as she yanks the waist of the leather pants she's attempting to squeeze me into.

"Sorry," she grumbles, only she doesn't sound sorry at all. She sounds irritated. "What size are you?"

"I'm a four who hasn't eaten in a month."

The wardrobe department, housed in a generously sized glass-paneled room, has transformed since the last time I was here. Rows of shiny chrome garment racks laden with clothes line the transparent walls, displaying the costumes and functioning as makeshift curtains.

When I had arrived yesterday, Ainsley's hands had been full setting up the space, so she gave me the choice.

Wait around or come back early afternoon today and run through all of it in a marathon session.

After my meeting with Wes left me both turned on and distressed, I bailed. While there's no way I can even consider sharing my feelings with him, my heart and hormones missed the memo.

Now, the price of my early escape is biting me in the ass. Since this morning, I've tried on dozens of outfits, excluding variations in accessories. I'm exhausted and, for me, who's always been self-conscious about comparisons to my twin, distressed.

"Damn, these are cut tight through the thighs." Ainsley tugs at me as if I were nothing but a store mannequin.

"No kidding," I reply.

She takes a few moments to study my abused thighs and ass. "Do me a favor?" she asks.

"Sure," I say, struggling to ignore my discomfort.

"When I pull up, I want you to jump a little."

"Are you serious?"

"Yes, but don't let your feet leave the ground."

"Jump, but keep my feet on the ground? What?"

"Just… start to go up on your toes, but don't actually leave the ground. We can both be injured. Or damage the outfit. That would be a colossal disaster."

"Sure would. We wouldn't want the pants to get hurt." My voice is sarcastic.

Ainsley mutters something unintelligible, then slides her thumbs inside the waistline of my pants and grips them.

"Ready?" she asks.

I nod, tighten my stomach, and grab the wall. "Yeah."

"Okay. Here we go." She takes a deep breath. "One, two… three!"

She tugs as I lift up onto my toes, throwing the force of my body up while she pulls the pants onto my hips. When we're done, the tight leather pants cling to me like the second skin they've become.

"Damn," Ainsley gasps, checking out my ass, then smooths the flesh around my waist with a lightly oiled hand. "Pure torture, but so worth it."

"That's what you think," I protest.

"Raelynn is no more than a two," Coraline, Raelynn's personal stylist chortles from across the room. Now that Ainsley's done pouring me into these pants, she tears herself away from texting and inspects the outfit.

"Now that we've got the pants onto Rose's ass," she remarks with a critical tone as she glares at my thighs, "we can finally start."

"Thirty-five, twenty-four, thirty-five." I return her bitch-glare with one of my own. "Get a tape measure if you want. My ass isn't going anywhere. Work with it… or don't."

Coraline's eyes meet mine with a calm nod, a sign that she's picked up on my deeper dare. *Go ahead, complain to my twin sister. See how far it gets you.*

My sister met Coraline when she first moved to LA, before she was famous. They'd worked together on shoots, and when Raelynn hit it big, she hired Coraline to be her personal stylist.

But as much as Coraline worships Raelynn, she loathes me. When I started my job as Rae's PA, Coraline treated me as if I worked for her too. She made my life miserable whenever she could and constantly reminded me that I wasn't in Raelynn's league.

I knew that. But modeling was never my goal, and it wasn't her place to punish me for it.

Twins don't like being compared, and that day I insisted that Coraline's mistreatment of me was over, one way or another. If Raelynn felt Coraline's fashion sense was essential to her brand, well, there were plenty of other assistants out there. Despite the up-and-downs, I missed my own career.

My sister's last assistant stole thirty-five grand from her, and she refused to go through that again. I don't know what she told Coraline, but now she behaves with more self-restraint. I've also learned over time that most bullies dislike you because somehow you cause their own insecurities to fester.

While Coraline possesses a highly deserved reputation for her fashion sense and is extremely well-styled herself, she's not physically attractive, at least not in this industry. She's short with a round figure and sharp features that give her a hawkish, harsh look.

Now I understand that she detests me because I lack the desire to be part of a world where she strives to be relevant. Every day, I squander a gift she'd kill to have, and she hates me for it.

Coraline doesn't know that I hate my job as much as she hates me, but the day I leave we'll both be in happier places.

She walks around me, carefully studying the outfit, the same way she's been doing all day. Coraline touches the smooth planes of my stomach, ensuring that the flesh won't spill out over the waistband. She runs her fingers along the double stitched side seam running down my outer thigh before inspecting my rear end.

"Impressive," she declares. "Smoking hot. These are keepers for Raelynn, if there aren't other objections."

"Other objections?" I groan. "Who else needs to weigh in?"

"Anyone with creative input or final approval," Ainsley replies. "Us, the director, and the producer."

"Wes Anders?" I ask.

"Probably the whole band, since they've self-financed this production."

"Oh." This information surprises me. It also explains Wes's hands-on approach with everything. "When does this all happen?"

Ainsley pulls a phone from her rear pocket. "Five minutes. Leave these pants on and wear those shoes and halter top." She gestures to a nearby table. "Let's go backward from there. Otherwise, you'll have to take off and put them on again."

"Please, no."

"Where are we doing this?" Coraline asks.

"Just outside here." Ainsley points to an exit in the back of the room. "It leads to the large atrium we use for our production meetings. Hopefully, we can get this done in an hour or two."

I stare up at the modern-looking analog clock next to the door. It's almost six. We've been here for hours, and I hoped to get off my feet for a while. A bathroom break would also be nice, but with these leather pants—that's out of the question.

"Ready?" Ainsley asks me.

"Sure," I say.

"Give me a minute to see if everyone's here."

Ainsley moves past clothes racks that line walls. A large white bulletin board is packed with notes, swatches, and accessories that block the glass and metal industrial door.

"Coraline, maybe you should join everyone?" Ainsley tells her as she rolls the board out of the way and props the door open with the lever at the bottom.

Through the door, I can see about six people. Some are talking, while the rest check their phones. On the far side of the room, Wes stands alone with his back against the wall, and an impatient scowl on his face.

His expression makes my stomach turn somersaults.

"Are we ready to start? Anyone else need to be here?" Ainsley asks.

Everyone pauses and looks around. Wes pushes himself off the wall and approaches the conference table in the front. He takes the center seat, and people spread out accordingly.

Next to Wes, a Vikingesque mountain of a man with a long, trimmed beard and tatted arms settles into his chair with a loud creak. Vince. We've never met, although word is he likes to raise hell given any chance. Jai sits on his other side. He introduced himself yesterday and he's super nice, easygoing, and all-around likeable.

A familiar character flanks Wes's other side. The mall-brand clothes, neat but unremarkable hair, and high-energy frazzled look scream PA. When he throws a messenger bag over his chair and tosses a pile of miscellaneous crap on the table, I'm positive this is Felix.

Coraline introduces herself to Wes, then takes the seat next to Felix and pulls out a tablet and stylus from her oversized purse. Wes looks around, notes a single empty chair, and clenches his jaw.

"Let's get started, Ainsley," he announces in a clear voice.

"Right away, Wes." Ainsley walks quickly out the industrial door to stand in front of the long table.

"You've all read the script. This is for the opening scene in the video *Wonderland: Pretty Little Liar*. This first outfit is what our 'Alice/Alicia' wears immediately before we flip the script on the audience."

"You mean just before she enters Wonderland?" Coraline asks.

"Exactly. Only in this video, our world is the crazy fucked up one. And Wonderland is, well... wonderful," Wes explains.

"Got it," Coraline answers, taking notes.

"Rosalie?" Ainsley calls to me. "We're ready for you."

The industrial light in the atrium is bright, as in it gives-me-a-headache bright. I take a deep, heavy breath and try to steady myself. This is so not my thing. As I struggle to suppress feelings of fear and resentment, I glance at Wes.

Mistake. Big, big mistake.

His faded jeans and motorcycle boots send blood rushing to my erogenous zones faster than Niagara Falls.

That long, blue-black hair is loose today, falling in waves down the back of his neck.

As I approach where everyone is seated, wearing sky-high heels, tight as hell leather pants, and a bandeau top with a tiny ruffle that skirts my ribcage in an inverted V, Wes's eyes widen and smolder.

He runs a hand through the long strands of hair and licks his lips. Those long legs stretch out beneath the table, and his hands rub the tops of his thighs. When our gazes meet, Wes's expression projects pure, predatory heat.

That's when I lose it.

Damn it, he knows.

He knows I'm not Raelynn, but he still looks at me like that.

Maybe it's all the stress, or the fact I haven't eaten or drank today. It could be the pounding headache from these bright interior lights, or the odd unsettled sensation that's been rooted in the pit of my stomach for the last month.

Whatever the reason, a tidal wave of nausea forcefully asserts itself. My physical discomfort and emotional distress act out together. A queasy light-headed sensation overtakes me and my knees buckle.

"Oh, for fuck's sake." Coraline's disgusted outburst is the last thing I hear before my face hits the floor.

CHAPTER EIGHTEEN

WES

"*S*he didn't slip, you idiot. She fainted," I tell the middle-aged dragon huffing impatiently at Rosalie's limp body on the floor. What's up with that stylist? Clara, Cora, or whatever her name is, strikes me as a bigger diva than many A-listers I know.

The shit you deal with when you're in charge.
Fuck me.

I race to Rosalie, where she lays unmoving a few feet in front of the table.

"Rose? Rose? Wake up, Rose." My fingers stroke her cheek, and she stirs.

Her hand covers mine, and she caresses it gently.
"Musician's hand," she murmurs, tracing the rough callouses of my strumming hand with her fingertips. It's

odd that she said that, but I've got other priorities
right now.

"Rose? Hon? Please…" I shake her gently.

All at once, she bolts upright, eyes wide open. Then
she groans and clutches her temples before peering around
the room.

"Hey there." I express a sigh of relief and smile.

"What… What happened?"

"You fainted," I explain. "How do you feel?"

"Sorry. Really, really sorry." Rose tries to stand but
collapses back onto the floor.

"Take it easy, Rose." I squeeze her shoulder to keep
her from falling over. "Someone get some water, please."

Beside me, Felix cracks the seal on a plastic bottle and
hands it over.

"Oh my God, I've put everyone so far behind." Rose
panics.

"Be quiet. Drink this. Come on." I dip the bottle near
her mouth and she takes it. When her hand touches me,
the rough callouses on her fingertips rub against my skin.
They're fresh, not dry or ragged, not shedding old surface
skin. They're alive, deep, ingrained.

Does Rose play an instrument too?

"Thanks. That's much better." She takes another
swallow.

"Rose, when's the last time you ate?" I ask.

"Lunch. Yesterday," she murmurs.

"That was pretty stupid." I can't hide my fury.

"It wasn't intentional. I just got busy and time
flew by."

"You're wearing too many hats on this production. We

need you to take care of yourself." It comes out harsher than intended.

"Look, I'm alright now. Let's finish this—"

"No. Hell no." I stand up to make an announcement. "That's a wrap for today, everyone. Felix will text you to reschedule. See you all tomorrow."

Around me the mood is mixed. There are sighs of relief, grumbles of irritation, and rapid movement out of the room. When they're gone, my attention turns back to Rose. Her expression is troubled and guilt-ridden.

I hate it.

"Wes, this is going to put you behind schedule."

"Don't worry about it. Darius never showed, so part of me wanted to cancel anyway. We'll deal with it tomorrow." I extend my hand down and she takes it in both of hers. I pull her up off the floor but don't let go right away.

Instead, my fingers trace the tips of hers, noting the pattern of the calluses and the slightly longer nails of her left hand.

"You know, a musicians' hands can say a lot about their music." I caress those delicate hands, silently begging them to tell me her secrets.

"That's true." Her voice is husky.

"You're a southpaw?" I ask.

"Yeah. Just like you."

I smile. "Guitar?"

"Not much lately, but yeah."

"I haven't played much either lately, and I'm a professional musician."

"Isn't it amazing how life gets in the way sometimes?"

Her words exude wisdom and sadness. Rose is

pensive, compassionate, kind. That's not to say her sister isn't, it's just... Wow.

If I'm honest, I don't know all that much about her sister, other than those aren't the qualities that come to mind when I think of Raelynn Tailor.

"Let me look at you." I smooth Rose's dark hair away from her face and over her shoulders. I tell myself it's only to check for cuts and bruises, but every curve, angle, and imperfection is committed to memory when I've finished.

It's like seeing her for the first time.

"Come on." I'm reluctant to let go. "Let's get something to eat and then I'll drive you home."

CHAPTER NINETEEN

ROSE

"*T*hat was nice. Thank you."

"Yeah, it was," Wes replies with an edge of surprise in his voice. "I'm glad you enjoyed it, and I hope you're feeling better."

"Exactly what I needed." It had never occurred to me to order a chirashi bowl without rice. The mix of premium vegetables and fish from one of our best local sushi bars has me feeling better since I began starving myself for this video production.

Of course, trading smiles over dinner with Wes has done more for my spirits than anything for ages.

Exhaustion hit us both like a ton of bricks when we sat down. Eventually, we discussed progress on the video, even traded some ideas.

All without a single mention of my sister.

I'm in the passenger seat of Wes's old school convertible as we travel through the surface streets back to my house. It's after eight and distant stars start to emerge under the cloudless sky. A faint breeze with the slightest edge of coolness flows over the open convertible top, just enough to feel good.

"Do you like being a PA?" he asks.

It seems like a random question, but he knows enough about me now that it doesn't make sense to him. Hell, most days it doesn't make sense to me.

The question elicits a bitter laugh. "That's a big hell no."

"Oh..." It's obvious I didn't give him the answer he expected. "Then how did you end up working for your sister?"

"It was one of those things." I breathe a frustrated sigh. "I'd lost my job, she'd just fired an assistant. It was supposed to be a temporary gig. Four years later, I'm still here. Not for long, though."

"You're quitting.?" he asks.

"Yeah." It's the first time I've said it out loud to anyone else. I've groaned about wanting to quit someday, but never in a 'this is going to happen now' way before. "When the Pretty Little Liar video is done, so am I."

"That's not much time. Do you already have a job, or will you quit and find one later?"

"I think this needs to be a hard reset." A sensation of calm overcomes me as the warm summer air stings my face and whips through my hair. Wes remains silent for so long, I wonder if our conversation is over.

"I hope your timing has nothing to do with our video."

"It played a part, but it wasn't the cause. I realized I've been waiting for a long time, telling myself that when things got better I'd leave. But…"

"But what?"

"I was lying to myself. I wanted to change my life while avoiding pain. Now I've let things reach the point where they're too painful to stay."

"I wouldn't have guessed you were so unhappy."

"Raelynn's life suits her better than it does me, as it should. But when you're twins, everyone assumes that we're interchangeable. That what she likes, I like." I give him a look of sad resignation. "But that's not always true."

"What don't you like?" As the light changes, we pass through the intersection and his focus returns to the road.

"The grueling schedule, the strict diet and exercise regimen that the video required, typical of any stand-in work. Then there's the sheer intrusiveness of it all." My stomach churns just thinking about it. "Raelynn's willing to endure all that in exchange for the money, opportunities, attention, and energy. I'm not, and it's impossible to avoid when my job is to manage those things for her."

Wes blows out a slow breath. When I glance over at him, he hesitates before speaking.

"Yeah, I'm not much into the attention either," he confesses.

"You? You play in sold out venues to tens of thousands of people."

"That's true. And I love the vibe that comes off a live crowd. For me, it's like a drug." He takes his eyes off the road to glance over at me. "But when it's over, I want to go someplace peaceful and just… decompress."

Wow.

"That is so not your reputation," I answer after a stunned paused.

"And it's a reputation that's well earned. Back in the early days, I tried everything at least once."

"Everything?"

Wes shoots me a smile laden with wolfish irony. "Everything. But the drugs and anonymous sex never distracted me the way it did others. Hedonism was more of a phase for me, thank God."

"Distracted you from what?"

He's quiet for a moment. The streetlights illuminate the interior of the car, and I watch his hands clench and unclench the steering wheel while a muscle in his lean cheek twitches. It's clear he's struggling with his answer. Wes takes a deep breath, then exhales before speaking.

"I hate pretty much everything about touring," he finally admits.

"Ahh!" A shocked, wordless gasp is my only response.

"Don't tell the fans," he pleads with a joking huff.

"Why do you hate it so much?"

"I don't hate everything. Music and live performances keep me sane. The synergy that comes from interactions with other musicians makes me feel… fulfilled. But a strange hotel bed every night, waking up in a different city every day without time to explore or meet anyone. That sucks for me. I'm either with throngs of strangers or the band. It's no secret Vince gets on my nerves. But those choices and loneliness are my only options on the road."

"Is that why Jester's Edge is financing this production? And why you're an executive producer?"

"You know about that?" he asks, surprised.

"Overheard some of the crew." I shrug.

"Partly. There are precious few ways musicians can make money for themselves. Live tours, paid appearances, merchandise sales, songwriting, and producing albums. Everything else is a cut of someone's piece of you."

"Do you need the money?" I'm shocked.

Wes laughs. "Life's good at the moment. But I'm close to thirty now and want to diversify. I also know that spending the rest of my life on an endless world tour to pay my bills won't work for me."

His comment puts in me in mind of so many older bands, some in their fifties and sixties or even older, who still tour... do they keep it up because they love live performances or to pay the bills?

We continue the rest of our ten-minute drive in silence. The car slows down as it pulls into the neighborhood, and Wes's Chevelle makes a clunk sound as it hits the dip at the bottom of the driveway and climbs the slight incline to the horseshoe pathway outside the front porch.

As we pull up, motion sensors activate, illuminating the entryway and nearby garage. Wes pulls to a stop and cuts the engine.

"Is Raelynn home?" he asks without looking at me.

I peer through the garage window at the roofline of her lime green Porsche Macan. "I think so."

"Are you okay? Do you need help?" he asks.

"I should be fine. Leaving work early and eating real food helped a lot."

"My pleasure." He pauses and studies me, amused. "You know, convertibles are great, but the wind can sometimes leave your hair standing on end."

"What?" I pull the sun visor down and stare at the vanity mirror. "Holy Shit! I look like Don King when he repped Mike Tyson! Why didn't you say anything?"

Wes chuckles at my comparison, then runs his fingers through my hair in an effort to help. "Truthfully, I didn't really notice until we were about to say goodnight."

I sit in the passenger seat stock-still as he pushes wisps away from my face and behind my ears. His fingers smooth the hair at my crown as his touch finds its way to my nape.

When he's done, he cups my chin in his hand and smiles. "Perfect."

Under his intense gaze, I feel my face flush red as heat creeps from my core to my forehead and back again. He's still touching me, so I know he's aware of my physical reaction to him.

What astounds me is his physical reaction. Wes's breathing changes. His hand leaves my chin as it skates down the flesh of my neck and throat, where it toys with the tender flesh at the point on my V-neck tee shirt. His expression is filled with heat and desire, but his touch stills with indecision.

The indecision doesn't last.

Distracted by his tender caress, I look up in time to see his full lips descend onto mine. His gentle pressure causes me to draw in a breath, and I still as Wes explores my lips with soft kisses.

This kiss is night-and-day opposite from the launch party. Those kisses were urgent, heated acts that consumed us both. This one's no less intense, but more tender and tentative, like a living thing, unsure of what it's becoming.

Through ragged breaths, his lips explore mine with small kisses and gentle bites on my gloss-stained flesh, encouraging me to open myself to him. My jaw slacks, my lips part to invite him in. Together we join in a tangle of teeth and tongues, tasting and exploring each other.

My body turns into his, the back of my head slides down the passenger door until it hits the armrest, while Wes's body descends on top of mine. He smells like a warm summer evening, with the vague scent of wildflowers, heat, and traces of a musky masculine soap.

Supporting our joint weight quickly becomes painful, and I wince and arch into Wes as I pull away from his kiss. When he pauses and looks down at me to see what's wrong, I blush as heat rushes up my spine.

He responds with a smile, then pulls me down.

"Oof," I gasp as my back lands on the long bench seat of Wes's vintage convertible. He stretches his long, muscular body over mine and lowers himself onto me. As his finger explores the contours of my ribcage and the delicate lace of my demi-cup bra from underneath the filmy fabric of my tank top, my leg hooks around the back of his thighs.

I cling to him, grateful for the excuse of sliding off the seat to clutch him all the more tightly. He reaches back to clutch my leg and touches the slick skin of my exposed thigh.

Wes stills.

The friction between our bodies pushed his jeans down the length of his groin until its large swell prevented further descent. Beneath him, my pelvis is wedged underneath the top of his naked hips, the only barrier between us is the damp, flimsy fabric of my floral skater skirt.

A slight shift of his large bulge, the tiniest adjustment of my lacy thong, and we'd be in a very different place, physically and emotionally.

I hold my breath as Wes raises himself up and straddles me on the long car seat, panting as he studies my disheveled clothes before wiping his mouth with the back of his wrist.

"I'm sorry," he says.

"For what?"

"We're in your sister's driveway," he points out.

"And you don't want her to see us like this?"

"Do you?" he asks.

I feel like the victim of a Gatorade dump that was mostly ice. If nothing else, tonight has taught me I'm not in control of myself around him. I'm good until we touch. But when we do... damn.

It hurts that he can turn it on and off like a switch. It makes me feel cheap and vulnerable.

"I'm not here to put on a show, but she's my sister, not my mother." I swallow hard. "What's the problem?"

Wes steps onto the floorboard, slides over to the driver's seat, then smooths his hair and clothes. He says nothing as he wipes his face in the rearview mirror before turning to me again.

"It's not you, it's me," he tells me.

"The greatest lie ever told." I pivot to a sitting position and curl my legs under me, my feet planted on the seat of his vintage collector's car. I don't give a shit.

"It's not a lie." He whispers. "There's lots going on right now. We both know it."

"Okay… so what?"

Wes blows a frustrated breath. "I like you, Rose. Maybe more than I realized at first. We're also working together. Not a great time to start something. Then there's your sister, which takes this to another level."

The only word I hear is sister before my temper spikes. "She has nothing to do with this!"

"Take it easy, Rose. She does, whether you like it or not." Wes runs a hand through his tousled black hair. "Raelynn doesn't want to be with me, and that's fine. But that's a far place from being okay with us together."

"It's not up to her, Wes." I turn my body to face him. "It's our decision."

"Yeah? Well, I don't want to come between you two and end up defending myself from both of you. No thanks."

"That's nothing but a big cop out." I reach for the door, but Wes grabs my shoulder.

"Really?" he taunts. "Have you told your sister you like me? In a horizontal mambo kind of way?"

"No." I bristle at his words. "And newsflash, Wes. I haven't told anyone that." Even Nikki assumed, I just didn't correct her.

"Now that's a damn lie." His voice is soft as he lets go of my shoulder and strokes my hair. "You told me just a few seconds ago. Back arched, legs wrapped around me, sinful mouth giving as good it as gets." He brushes my bottom lip with the pad of his thumb. "If I hadn't stopped, we'd be living out your high school dating fantasies."

"My dating fantasies?"

"Sex with a rock star in a classic convertible."

"Jocks were my go-to in high school," I snap.

"I played baseball, too."

"No wonder Raelynn thinks you're a horrible bore," I snap. As soon as the words are out, I regret them.

His self-confident smile melts into a firm line. "This is exactly what I didn't want to get caught between. Good-night, Rose."

"Go to hell, Wes." I say in a quiet, controlled tone.

I open the door and slide out of his car without shutting the door for fear I'll slam it and give him the satisfaction of seeing me lose my temper. As I ascend the walkway and reach the front door, I hear the controlled squeal of Wes's tires as he leaves the driveway.

I'm mad at both of us right now. At Wes, for taking a sweet, honest moment and stuffing it down the garbage disposal. Of course, me being the one to make my sister's opinion of him relevant and ruin the mood angers me most of all.

What sucks about that is telling Wes what she said, because I lacked the power to hurt him myself. Seriously, would it wound him at all if I called him that? Hell no.

In the darkness, I fumble for my keys. They're difficult to find behind the well of tears.

CHAPTER TWENTY

WES

*D*own the hill from Raelynn's house, there's a dead-end street that overlooks the city skyline. It's the perfect place for me to pull over and cut the engine.

I rip my tee shirt off and rub the silky thin fabric across my face, down the back of my neck and shoulders, then through my hair. Soon, the shirt smells like both of us. Vanilla, musk, mint, bergamot, honeysuckle, sweat.

When the material becomes dense with wetness, I twist it into a knot and throw it on the seat where Rose sat only moments ago.

Between unsteady breaths, my hands shake.

When Rose fainted, so many emotions had hit me. Protectiveness. Fear. Guilt. Anger. A swirling tsunami of angst overwhelmed me as I knelt next to her on the floor and begged her to wake up. Then when she was conscious again and volunteered to continue working, she made me feel like a selfish asshole.

Because I am a selfish asshole.

I've asked so much of her, depended too heavily on her, and offered little in return. Even worse, I denied what the hell was happening to us. To me.

Rose is likeable. From the moment we met, she's been a tell-it-like-it-is, straight-from-the-heart type of woman. Which is rare, especially in my social circles.

The day we arranged flowers together, when I realized who she was, my attraction had knocked me on my ass. But I'd denied it and told myself my hormones were confusing Rose with her twin sister. That was a lie, one I told myself more than once.

The same lie I told her tonight.

When Raelynn agreed to appear in the video, the days couldn't pass fast enough until her arrival. It's why I lied to myself and to Rose.

My night with Raelynn was wild, wicked, sponta-neous, unforgettable. How could she walk away and never look back? Until tonight, I've been obsessed with hearing her answer. Now, maybe I don't want to know.

From the cradle on the dashboard, my phone lights up with a new text.

It's Rose.

HER: *I'm sorry. I shouldn't have said that you were a bore.*

I scrub my fingernails through my hair and stare up at the moon.

> ME: *I shouldn't have been all over you.*
> HER: *Why?*
> ME: *Because I slept with your sister.*

There's a pause so long I think we're done. But as I get ready to start the car, my phone pings again.

> HER: *Does that matter to you?*
> ME: *Not much anymore. But that's not the point.*
> HER: *What is?*
> ME: *The fact that it clearly bothers you.*
> HER: *Not the way you think.*
> ME: *Why'd you tell me what she said? Why not call just call me an asshole?*
> HER: *You're right. I'm sorry.*
> ME: *It's more than that. I don't want to get between you two.*
> HER: *Trust me, that won't happen.*
> ME: *I can't. Not a big fan of Rae's right now. She ghosted me and fucked up our business arrangement with no explanation. And it's clear you haven't told her about your thing for me.*
> HER: *MAYBE I'm tired of everything being about her.*
> ME: *I get that. But you work for her, you live with her. Until you're ready for her to know, we've got a problem.*

I watch as the ellipse on my screen dances for a few moments and then finally disappears. Conversation over. While Rose's personal and professional life is tied to her sister, all our hang-ups will stay hung up. It sucks, but that's how it is.

If anyone had told me I'd live to regret sleeping with Raelynn Tailor, I'd have said they were crazy.

But sometimes crazy's all that's left.

CHAPTER TWENTY-ONE

ROSE

"If I get an erection, I'm sorry," Wes whispers.

"Got it, thanks. Anything else?" I reply.

"Yeah. If I don't get one, I'm sorry, too."

"Stop talking, Wes."

"Right."

"Quiet everyone!" the assistant director yells.

You'd assume from the solitary intimacy of the final cut that a love scene made during a professional production would be created under tranquil conditions. In reality, production proceeds with all the chaos and comfort you'd expect from a pelvic exam in the middle of an ER during a pandemic.

"Wes, try to center your right hands' grip on her breast, please," Darius instructs.

"He needs to keep his hands on the pasties as much as possible," Millicent tells Darius.

"Hear that, Wes? Keep your hands on the silicone cutlets."

How was I ever worried that my physical attraction to Wes would run away with me on the set?

Wes stands behind me, shirtless, with a pair of low slung faded blue jeans that reveal the ridgeline of his hips. Each of his hands holds one of my breasts, which he's been doing with moderate variations for over an hour.

We started out with more tepid poses, but as we've moved through the shoot, our poses have steadily become more heated as Darius meticulously captures each from several angles.

Of course, that achievement requires an entire squad, adding to the intimacy of the set. There are at least three lighting guys here, some ambiguous crew, a sound guy with the boom microphone. Further back from Wes are the camerawoman and her assistant. Darius and his assistant are close, too, with Millicent next to him.

If the crowd wasn't big enough, everyone who showed up brought a friend. Off to the side, Vince and Jai watch with intensity, while Felix and Nikki stand around with time on their hands.

What's the big attraction? Me, I think.

Maybe I'm just self-conscious standing here in my favorite leather pants, topless. Topless, except for these giant silicone cutlets taped over my nipples and fastened to my naked skin with long strips of surgical tape high on my chest. No doubt the perfect flesh colored plumpness will enhance my natural lack of cleavage in post-production.

"… and cut! That's a wrap. Everyone, take thirty minutes for lunch."

My body sags with relief. Millicent approaches me with a long, thin bathrobe which she tosses over my shoulders. I tie it tight around my waist, grateful for the coverage. After adjusting the robe, I turn and look for Wes.

By the time I spot him, he's halfway to the exit, still shirtless. Felix scurries behind and offers him a dark tee-shirt. Wes takes it from him and throws it over his head, pulling it down without breaking stride, then disappears out the door. Well, I guess he's able to manage our physical chemistry without breaking a sweat, but then again, what else is new?

"Nice work this morning," Millicent tells me. "When we get back from lunch, I'll retape your breasts for the afternoon."

"Retape? Oh, I'm looking forward to it." My tone is sarcastic as I roll my eyes. "Thank you, Millicent. I really am very grateful you're here." I give her a sincere smile. I wasn't sure how this was going to work out, but you and Wes were right."

The thought of some random intern helping to tape up my boobs makes me cringe.

"I get it, and you're welcome. Don't know if I'd rather kiss or curse at the people who invented that heavy duty adhesive tape," she replies.

"Have a good lunch," I tell her.

Millicent waves at me, then nods at Nikki as she

approaches me with a large disposable coffee mug.

"Hey, girl." Nikki offers the mug as she greets me.

"Thanks for showing up," I say. "Raelynn's not keeping you busy?"

"She tries. But truthfully, I think she's holding back until you 're done here. Heads up."

"Great." I take a sip of the coffee. It leaves a strange aftertaste. "Nikki, what it is this?"

"Milton's black coffee… with a few scoops of protein powder. How is it?"

"Just shoot me now." I reply.

"Are you sure you don't want to eat something?" she asks.

"I'd love to, but not until we're done for the day. If I bloat up, these pants will be even more uncomfortable than they are already." I take another sip of coffee and try to ignore the bitter aftertaste. "This is fine."

"Speaking of fine." Nikki pauses to look around. "How are things with Wes?"

"Strained. But we're both easy to distract with work and hard deadlines."

"Well, if you're that into each other, maybe you should tell him the truth."

"No way."

"Why not?" she asks.

I look around the deserted studio. No doubt everyone ran to the caterer's spread for their break. Being alone makes it an easy choice to confide in Nikki.

"Because I'm tired of being compared to Raelynn and coming up short. I can't go through that with Wes."

"Why do you always think that will happen? Some of

us with souls and sense wouldn't draw a different conclusion."

"Because it's already happened," I confess.

Nikki looks around again and lowers her voice. "What has?"

"We kissed. Again. Last night in his car, like a pair of sexually frustrated teenagers."

"Wow. And then what?"

I don't know if it's the crazy crap in the coffee or the memory that upsets me, but suddenly I'm sick to my stomach. "He stopped cold because he was worried Raelynn would see us."

Nikki's eye narrow in confusion. "Um, ah… where were you?"

"In the circular driveway in front of Raelynn's front porch." I shrug. "It was a spontaneous goodnight kiss that got a little… heated."

"That's just messed up."

"I know." Deep down inside, it's fair to say I hope Wes figures out that it's me he was with the night of the launch party. Rae and I are twins, but we're not that inter-changeable… right? It's strange that I'm okay with Wes accusing me of deception, while being reluctant to confess.

Am I selfish or just human?

"There could be several reasons he doesn't want your sister to know. Your personal lives and business are all wrapped up too tight. You, Wes, Raelynn, none of you have any extra capacity at the moment. Be careful. If you don't want to tell him about the launch party, you better make damn sure someone else doesn't."

"Like who?"

"Start with who else knows."

"Me, you. Oh, and Huey my sister's bodyguard, but he would never say anything. He signed an NDA."

"And Raelynn," she reminds me. "Don't forget about Raelynn."

"If only that were possible," I reply.

CHAPTER TWENTY-TWO

WES

"*L*et's discuss the kiss," Darius says. He gestures for us to join him on the set.

"Long. Slow. Hot… think you can manage that?" Darius looks back and forth between Rose and me. "Are your Zombiesque responses a yes or no?"

Roses' face stiffened into a bitch-mask at the word kiss. My own jaw throbs from trying to remain stoic and professional. This entire morning has been hell for me and Rose.

We haven't discussed what happened last night, which says a lot about the situation between us. Spending the morning half-naked while we filmed only added to our unresolved tension.

And the worst is yet to come. Darius has legitimate worries.

"Sure," Rosalie replies. "Not a problem."

"Fabulous news." Darius nods in approval. "Wes? It's your show."

"Let's get started then," I reply.

As everyone else gets to their positions, Rose and I walk onto the set. There's no opportunity to speak, as Millicent approaches us to take Rose's robe. She pulls the robe off Rose's shoulders, and she turns to face me, naked from the waist up except for the cutlets. I focus on her collarbone, but the skin there quickly flushes pink. The wave of warm color sends a jolt of heat down my spine.

"Hey, Rose's skin tone changes at the neckline. What gives?" Darius complains.

"It's the lights," Rose and I answer at the same time.

"Make-up, please," Darius says. "Let's tone her down."

A man with tatted arms appears with flesh-colored powder and smooths it along her jawline, then blends it down her neck and along the upper ridge of her collarbone, then arranges strands of Rose's long blonde wig around her face. By the time he's done, I've pulled it together, while Rose exhales.

"Let's get some poses before the kiss. Wes, go right, hands on her upper arms. Rose left, both hands on the waist of his jeans."

"Quiet on set," the assistant director announces.

"Cameras speeding. Pretty Little Liar, second verse. Camera one behind Wes, take one. Pretty Little Liar, second verse. Camera two behind Rose, take one. Pretty

Little Liar, second verse. Take one. Camera three, center front."

"Audio rolling. Slate," the camera assistant says. A moment later, "Clean slate."

"Action," Darius says.

We do several short takes with our heads at multiple angles and hands in different positions, and that's when our undeniable chemistry makes its presence known. Rose and I become hyper-attuned to one another's movements and start to predict each other, which makes the scenes flow with incredible authenticity.

When Darius yells 'cut,' Rose and I move away from each other as fast as possible without running. It's... painful to be so close, half-dressed, and try to stay detached, especially with so much unresolved sexual tension between us. She tucks into her robe, and the make-up artist touches up her face.

Off set, near the back exit, I slide down the wall and sit on the hard floor, then reach into the coin pocket of my jeans and insert a two-thousand-dollar pair of Bluetooth earbuds. The noise cancelling on these is incredible and the Bluetooth taps into the *Pretty Little Liar* audio that the crew uses to sync the scenes. In mere moments, I'm off in my own world, taking a well-needed break.

All the things that pretty little liars do,
I'm gonna do to you.
Pout and shout, kiss and cry,
Form crazy thoughts that never die,
Twisted feelings that won't not hurt,
I'll take them out on you.
All. Over You.

And those things you did to me,
I'm gonna do to you.
Pretty little liar.

"Hot set," one of the crew announces.

Now that the set configuration is complete, we'll go back to filming soon. If I don't return, they'll send someone to find me, which means this quiet spot won't remain hidden. Reluctantly, I stand and head back to the set, where I consciously seek out Rose.

She's leaning against the wall farthest from the set. Her long body arched, head back, eyes closed, throat exposed. Watching the knot at the slender v of her neck reminds me of how pink it turned when I stared at her.

It's like she can feel me watch her, because her eyes open with a sudden start and she pushes herself off the wall and looks around. When I wave at her, she bobs her chin at me, then tightens the belt of her robe.

"Last looks!" The assistant director says.

The tattooed makeup artist approaches me with a set of brushes. Looking me over, he reaches into his black apron and pulls out several tubes and mixes the contents of on the back of his hand before smearing it across my cheeks and the bridge of my nose. When he's done, he gives me a gentle dust of flesh-colored powder.

"Thanks," I tell him.

He nods wordlessly, then disappears.

"Quiet, please," says the assistant director.

Around the set, people take their positions on the

production, including Rose and I. Darius meets us on the set and gives us his final directions.

"Remember. Slow. Long. Hot. If this goes well, it should be our last scene today."

I'm vaguely aware of the crew confirming their status with one another. In front of me, Rose straightens her shoulders and stiffens before removing her robe. Even though she's got a killer bod, my eyes don't leave her face.

If she's uncomfortable without her robe, it no longer shows. Instead, she's focused on the scene, Darius' instructions, and doing the best she can. When she smiles palms up in a silent ask for permission to touch me, my draw drops into a speechless nod. As Rose's hands settle onto my naked waist, I grasp her upper arms and tilt my head down to hers.

"Action," Darius says.

I brace myself for the inevitable rush that tears through me as my mouth brushes her soft, gloss-coated lips. It comes hard and fast, the way it did in the car last night, when we went from a simple kiss to me straddling her on the front seat of my car. There's an unresolved, untapped chemistry between us that refuses to be checked when we're in physical contact.

Rose's self-control dissipates. Her body arches into mine, and the heated skin of her torso rubs against mine. My hands wander through the hair of her wig, down that taut, naked back, finding her hips, pressing them against mine

This feels good. Really good, and not in a torqued and tempted way. It's... familiar. Too familiar. The muted smell of vanilla and heat. The way she turns her neck when I stroke her hair. How the pads of her fingers rub the exposed ridge of my pelvis that tickles and arouses me all at once.

I want to explore, keep going, understand this connection we share, but Rose's hands encircle my neck, pulling me away from those pouty lips of hers.

"Wes," Rose rasps between kisses. "Wes? Please. Wes!"

I pull away from her and stare down at her stunned expression. She blinks fast several times.

"What?" I ask, looking around the set.

People are staring. As in jaws dropped, hands-over-mouth staring.

"What happened?" I ask Rose.

"Um, the director said 'cut.' Like three times," she says.

"Are you okay, Rose?" Darius asks.

She nods.

"Excuse me," Millicent appears, and with her back to me, covers Rose with a bathrobe.

I look up at Darius, who's half out of his chair with his hands raised. "What the hell, Wes?" he asks.

Fuck. I reach up and click my earbud off button. "I didn't hear you," I explain to Rose as much as Darius. "I'm wearing my earbuds." I look around the set. "The speakers are off, but the music is still playing."

"Cut the music! All of it! Everywhere!" Darius thunders. Off to the side, a kid wearing an intern lanyard and a terrified look on his face snaps a switch on the control board. But before Darius can hoist his head on a spit, he turns his attention to back to me.

"Why are you wearing those? There's no lip-synching in this scene."

"I used them during the break. That song's been playing all day. When it started back up, I didn't notice. It hasn't stopped playing, they just cut sound to the speakers."

"Well, damn, Wes, I'd bitch to the producer, but we know how far that would get me. No earbuds unless the sound department gives them to you and there's lip synching scenes on the call sheet."

"It won't happen again," I say, then turn to Rose. "I'm so sorry. Are you okay?"

"Yeah." She sounds a little breathless. "A bit confused at first, but I get it now."

"That makes one of us," I reply.

"Excuse me?"

"I don't get this." I feel a sudden wave of confused exhaustion come over me. "We keep telling ourselves and each other that. But then this happens."

"I'm sorry," she whispers.

"No. No, I don't want you to be sorry." My voice quiets so only she can hear me. "I want us to talk. About us. No pretense about anything else. Please? You know it's important. This can't keep happening."

"Okay," she nods.

"Good. I've got to deal with today's rushes. After that last scene it's urgent."

"Um… too much information," she jokes.

I laugh. No one else heard our exchange, but everyone around me seems to relax, including Rose.

"Get your mind out of the sewer. Rushes, the unedited footage from today."

"Right. I knew that."

"Of course." My voice becomes serious. "Felix will come find you."

CHAPTER TWENTY-THREE

ROSE

"Where are we going?" I ask. Felix leads me to the parking lot and beside the studio.

"Not far," he insists.

He texted me this morning and asked me to meet him by the door next to the parking lot instead of entering the building, he steered me around the side to a massive luxury RV. It's parked alongside the studio and must be forty feet long.

"What is this?" I ask.

"The band's home away from home." Felix pauses at the front door. "This is where Wes comes when he works round the clock and needs to decompress or not be interrupted."

"It's seven thirty and I'm not a morning person. I really need a coffee and a few minutes to drink it."

"You're covered. I made some this morning." Felix knocks loudly on the RV door. When there's no answer, he removes a key from his pocket and unlocks it before holding the door slightly ajar and thrusting his head through the opening.

"Hello, hello? Guys? Anybody here? It's Felix. I have Rosalie Tailor with me." When no one answers, Felix holds the door open, steps inside, and gestures for me to follow.

"Help yourself." He points to a coffee pot on the counter, then moves to the back of the RV.

Several gigantic mugs line the counter, and I pour myself a large helping of rich smelling java and a generous portion of vegan creamer. It's not half-and-half, but it's good enough to pretend.

I take a much-needed gulp and enjoy the warm rush that fills my body and jump starts my senses. When the fog clears, my thoughts turn to Wes and what he wants to discuss.

It's clear we're attracted to each other. Really, really attracted. Yesterday, I tried so hard to focus on my performance and be professional. The harder we both try to stay in neutral, the more we... don't.

Our attraction aside, I like him a lot. Wes isn't the jerk my sister implied he was. But I refuse to get Raelynn's permission to be with him. I can't do it.

Troubled, I look for a distraction and take in my surroundings. At first it feels intrusive, being in someone else's house when they're gone. But it soon becomes clear that while the RV is as luxurious as a five-star hotel, it's also sterile and lacking in personal items.

Except for an open composition book on the coffee table.

Musical notes scrawled in bright blue ink over rich black staff lines etched into cream-colored paper call to me like a siren. I'm trying to read them upside down when Felix returns.

"Rose?" His voice makes me jump.

"Yeah?"

"I texted Wes. He's putting out a fire and wants to know when your first meeting is today?"

"Eight fifteen."

"Felix's thumbs punch his phone with a rapid rhythm. A few moments later, it buzzes with Wes's response.

"Wes says he needs about ten minutes and wants you to wait for him here." Felix looks up from his phone.

"Okay."

He taps something into his phone but doesn't wait for a response. Seconds later, it vibrates again. "Gotta go, Rose. Later."

After Felix leaves, my attention turns back to the open notebook on the coffee table. I'm wildly curious but hesitant too. Music is an art form, like drawing or writing. It can feel wrong for someone to look at if you're not ready to share. But surely, whoever wrote it wouldn't have left the book wide open on the coffee table if its contents were a closely guarded secret?

When the guitar leaning against a chair next to the coffee table comes into view, curiosity gets the better of me and I take a seat and hoist it into my lap. It's an old beat-up acoustic with deep gouges in the face and faded paint along the band.

I give it a tentative strum. It's in perfect tune, and to my delight, strung for a southpaw. We're encouraged to play right-handed when we take music lessons, but if you're like me and self-taught before being schooled, it's practically impossible to switch later.

My parents gifted me guitar lessons for my fifteenth birthday, but by then I'd been self-teaching on a used guitar since my tweens. After years of YouTube videos, my teacher gave up on me playing right-handed by our second lesson.

I loved music, dreamed of Nashville and no longer needing to share a room with Raelynn. As the reality of my situation washes over me, my fingers strike a sour note.

But that doesn't stop me. It never has and never will.

My fingers dance across the strings, playing my regular warm up, and I can feel the muscles and tendons in my hands become more pliable with every note. After a few moments, my whole body relaxes. I'm eager to play something, anything, and that's when I glance back at the open composition book.

I slide it across the table and study the notes. It's a rough draft of a song. There are long bars filled with strings of notes, but some portions are crossed out, with musical notes scribbled along the margins in smeared ink. The smears and crowded symbols make it hard to 'hear' the melody in my head, so I start to hum, but it's not as intuitive for me.

Annoyed, I pull the composition close and begin to

play. The opening chords are deceptively simple, but it gets more complicated as elements are added in later progressions. It's beautiful but incomplete, so I take the score in different directions until one works for me.

Then I do what comes naturally, adding lyrics to the measures.

All I never wanted; you are all I ne-ve-ever wanted. Ne-ev-er wanted.

> *It's nighttime now, but I'm still awake.*
> *My covers are damp, my memories dank,*
> *Of that time in my life when we shared so much,*
> *Infectious laughter, you're incredible touch.*
> *Until we didn't, and you left me alone.*

All I never wanted, all I never wanted. You're all I never wanted.

> *I don't want to feel that feeling again,*
> *Of not being loved like I did back then,*
> *The sleepless nights and unanswered texts*
> *And lonely mornings filled with regret.*

All I never wanted, all I never wanted. You're all I never wanted,

> *Now you come back,*
> *You're sorry, you say*
> *That you were a fool,*
> *Today's a new day,*

And you want to live by different rules.
Doesn't it suck to be so cruel?
All I never wanted, ne-e-ver wanted,
The hope that comes before a fall—

"All I never wanted. You are a-l-l I've always wanted. Doesn't it suck to be so cruel, to be so cruel? Doesn't it hurt to be made a fool?"

I bolt up in my seat as another voice repeats the refrain of the song and starts to improvise.

It's Wes.

That smooth, incredible baritone stands out in all modern music. Distinct, timeless, haunting, powerful yet vulnerable. I close my eyes and listen to him get a feel for my lyrics, play with them, repeat and change, add new ones, then test them. There's no degradation in tone or vocal quality, even up close.

"Not bad. What do you think?" he asks.

"I think that if archangels spoke, they'd sound like you," I answer.

"Aww, looks like somebody likes you, Wes," another voice answers.

My eyes fly open, and a flush of heat creeps up my spine when it becomes clear Wes isn't alone. He's with Vince. And he wasn't asking for my opinion.

Shit.

"Sorry," I gasp and stand.

"Don't be," Wes insists. "I asked you to meet me here." He side-eyes Vince as he speaks.

Beside him, Vince clears his throat. "I'm Vince. It's probably time for us to meet."

"Guess there wasn't a reason up until now. I'm Rosalie Tailor."

"Raelynn Tailor's twin sister." Vince gives me an assessing look. "You must be the pretty one."

"Vince, ease up already," Wes says.

"What? I thought you were into her sister."

"That's none of your business."

"It is if you're telling me to back off. Unless you've got some kind of menage thing going on…?"

I gasp in disgust.

"Vince, stop upsetting her," Wes warns him.

"Upset her? What?" Vince insists. "Are you upset, Rose?"

It's my turn to level a death-glare. "Vince? Go to hell."

Vince laughs out loud. "Fair enough. Once up on a time, Wes was up for anything. You?" He nods toward the guitar in my hands. "You're pretty good for an amateur."

"Who said I was an amateur?" I ask.

"You're not?"

"No. But I'm a composer, not a performer."

"Well, damn. You should come sit in with us at Wes's tomorrow night." Vince nudges Wes. "Right?"

"You want me to hang out with Jester's Edge while you work?" I give him the mother of all eye rolls.

"Why the hell not? You said you were a pro. With the hellish week we've had, I doubt we'll do much actual work. Right, Wes?"

"That's up to Rose," Wes answers.

"I'll leave you two to sort it out." Vince yawns and stretches. "It's too early for me and I'm going to sleep it off until my next appointment. Nice meeting you, Rose. Hope we can talk later without a chaperone."

Vince turns toward the back and pulls his tee shirt off as he walks to the back room, putting his cut back and arms on display.

"Asshole," Wes mutters after Vince closes the bedroom door behind him.

"Wow," I blink. "Is he always that over the top?"

"Believe it or not, plenty of women find him a big turn on."

"When the stampede starts, let me know so I can jump out of the way," I say.

He nods in solemn promise.

CHAPTER TWENTY-FOUR

WES

"*H*ow do you like my guitar?" I ask.

"This is yours?" Her eyes widen like saucers before she sets the guitar down, careful to avoid banging it against the chair frame. "You're the last person I thought would own this."

"Why?" I'm curious.

"It's acoustic. You play electric on stage. It's also beat up. You're low key but not low-brow." She looks down at it again. "But... I realize now that it's like you in one critical sense."

"Really?"

"Yeah. You both sound incredible." She shakes her head and flushes a pretty pink color. "I know it seems like a gushy, girlie, groupie thing to say, but it's true, and I mean it sincerely." She takes a breath. "I'll stop talking now."

"Oregon spruce and myrtle wood," I say.

"That explains it," she replies. "The guitar anyway."

She's flustered, so I ignore her compliment. Instead, I pick up the guitar and strum.

"This was my first real guitar. It was a present, bought used for eight hundred dollars by my grandfather." I laugh at the memory. "My parents thought he was nuts."

"Grandparent's rock," she replies. "My grams financed my first one with a larger than average birthday card. A few years later, my parents caved and gave me music lessons."

"You're a musician." I nod toward the couch and she sits down. "Why didn't you say so sooner?"

Rosalie pulls her knees chestward on the couch. "My first foray into the profession wasn't exactly ground-breaking."

"Neither was mine." She gives me a questioning look, but I don't want to change the subject right now. "What happened?"

She hesitates while she peels the nude nail polish off her thumb. "Back in San Diego, I majored in musical composition. After a summer internship here, a production company hired me out of school to help compose, score, and arrange original music for a sci-fi fantasy series commissioned by a major streaming service."

Wow. She must be a serious talent to snag a gig like that.

"That sounds great," I say. "What happened?"

"The streaming company decided that they'd done

enough Zombie apocalypse shows. Six months later, it was over."

"Having your first big gig go down in flames can be demoralizing."

She looks up at me, her expression a mixture of pain, shame, and insecurity.

"Where'd you work next?" I ask.

"For Raelynn." She stares back down at the coffee table. "I moved in with her just as her modeling career took off. She needed help. It's been that way ever since."

Every time Rose and I have a conversation, another layer gets peeled back, revealing something that stuns me. When she mentioned her plans to quit working for her sister, it didn't sit well with me, because Rose was my connection to Raelynn, a choice that I didn't want anymore but still took bizarre comfort in its existence.

I strum my guitar and start to play simple chord progressions. It helps me process all she's told me. Across from me on the couch, Rose's posture relaxes. She stretches her long legs out onto the floor, and her arms relax, while her fingers tap out the chords I play on her knee.

In that mix of music and wordless silence, a realization occurs.

"Rose?"

"Mmm?" she replies, continuing to tap out notes on her knee.

"Remember when you told me you wanted to find another job and quit working for Raelynn?"

"Yeah?"

"You didn't mean another PA job, did you?"

"No," she stills again. "I intend to resume my music career. I've put it off long enough."

"Good for you."

My fingers, stretched and warm, glide over the guitar strings and a cacophony of melodies in my head take form as the physical constraints of the guitar force them into an order that allows their expression.

Beside me, Rose closes her eyes, resumes tapping her fingers and hums, harmonizing my melody, adding texture and complexity to it. When I pause, she takes the melody in a new direction that sounds like me... only better.

We do this exchange several times until we've got almost enough for an entire song. It's nothing short of incredible. Jester's Edge has great musical synergy, but it took a while to blend our styles, personalities, and preferences.

With Rose, it's instant synergy. We stop playing and humming at the same time and break into stunned, happy laughter.

"That was fun," she says. "You're lucky to get to do that every day."

"I know. And when you're with the right people, there's nothing better. Do you write lyrics?"

"Words come to me whenever I compose, but it's just part of my process. I don't write them down or anything."

"You should." I tell her. "Just record them on your phone."

"I'll think about it." She doesn't sound convinced.

"You should also come hang out with the band tomorrow night at my place."

Rose pulls her knees to her chest and hugs them close. "I don't think that's a good idea."

"Then let me say I'm sorry so you have time to rethink it."

"Apologize? You? For what?"

"The other night."

"Don't go there, Wes." Rose throws her hands into the air and stands. "Just don't."

"What? Wait!" I jump to my feet and stand in front of her. "What the hell did I say?"

Rose's demeanor does a total one-eighty. Both hands land on her waist while her hips jut into a defiant stance. Those cherry red lips that were such a pleasure to kiss the other night twist into an angry scowl. And I swear those electric blue eyes turn a hostile shade of grey.

"Let me guess. The other night was a mistake. You got a little carried away and it shouldn't have happened. Because despite you being ghosted by her, you've still got a thing for my sister."

Rose's voice is constrained and ragged, like she wants to shout but struggles for control. I watch with regret as she pinches her temples between her thumb and ring finger and squeezes.

"You've got it all wrong, Sweet Rose." My hands grasp sad, slumped shoulders. When our eyes meet, I gently shake her. "Hello? Perfectly lucid here. I know who I kissed. No regrets."

"Then why are you sorry?" Rose sounds both confused and incredulous.

"Because it was wrong for me to tell you how to handle your sister and what she thinks of your... our... us."

This conversation is painful and liberating. "I like you. A lot, Rose. The last thing I want is to make life more difficult, especially between the two of you. But... this isn't up to me."

"No," she agrees. "It's not."

I press a long kiss into her forehead, and she responds by wrapping her arms around my waist.

"I'm a control freak in my work. This isn't a secret. But I trust you, with this and however you want to handle your sister."

As I kiss the hop of her forehead, she shudders beneath me.

"Come hang us with us tomorrow night. But only if you want, no pressure."

She nods against my chest. "I should go," she says.

"Right." I let go, and her hands slide away. "See you later?"

Rose walks to the door of the RV and pushes it open. "Bye," she says.

Just like that, she's gone. And there's something familiar and unsettling about that sensation.

CHAPTER TWENTY-FIVE

ROSE

*T*he set-up is perfect.

The entire lower level of Wes's house revolves around music. A professional recording studio with a soundproof door and huge window overlooks a large sitting area equipped with stools, couches, and end tables with the occasional beer bottle or (in my case) glass of wine. It's the perfect way to spend a Friday evening after an intense week.

"What do you think, Rose?" Vince asks me from behind his drums.

He beats out the slow, steady rhythm of a song we've been working on for the past few hours. When he finishes one measure, I join in with my guitar, layering in melody as I try to understand the song we're creating together.

As yet, nothing's written, although now everyone seems to be headed in the same direction. For the first hour, I admit I felt intimidated. Who wouldn't be, sitting in with one of the most successful bands working today?

But after a while, it became too hard not to play. And too damn much fun once I started. As I coax the melody and start the second measure, the song speaks to me, like they usually do, and I translate it into words.

The door slams shut
In that just-so way.
I already know it's been a bad day.
Like most are lately.

My voice can hold its own, but beyond that it's unremarkable now. Throughout high school I sang with anonymity in the choir. Since my passions lie in arrangement and composition more than vocal performance, I made my peace with how things turned out long ago. Besides, when Wes Anders sings... everyone sounds like background noise.

Jai, Vince, and I repeat the first measure on our instruments while Wes sings my random lyrics.

The door slams shut
In that just-so way.
I already know it's been a bad day.
Like most are lately.

It's a rush to hear anyone, let alone Wes, sing my lyrics. It's like hearing the words for the first time. Lyrics are part of my composition process and when I hear them sung aloud, they supply inspiration for another verse:

It's no one's fault,
It never is, but sometimes there's
Just nothing left to give.
Nothing left to give.
Tell me you want me,
Don't drive me away.
If you want me to be here,
Then ask me to stay.

I repeat the last few bars on my guitar. "Not... bad," I answer Vince.

My gaze skates around the room, catching a collective nod from Jai, Vince, and Wes. They slouch in unison, and I soon learn that means we're done for the night.

Jai breaks the silence first. "I've gotta bounce, guys. It's late," he says, nodding at the wall clock.

"Turning in early?" Vince asks. "You're the youngest, but you're becoming an old man the fastest."

"Who said I was going home?" Jai asks.

"Well, okay then." Wes laughs.

Jai gives a non-committal shrug. "Rose, do you need a ride home?"

"I can take her," Vince interrupts. "Besides, you've got big plans, right?"

"Thanks, guys, but I was planning on getting an Uber." Nikki needed the Prius to run errands for Raelynn today.

"There's no need. I'll take you," Wes says. "If you've got time now, I'd like to play back the stream-of-conscious lyrics you came up with while we worked on the new music. They're a lot better than you realize."

"You think?" I ask.

"Yeah," Jester's Edge answers in unison.

Wow. It's been ages since I've worked with professional musicians, and it's gratifying that my work is well received.

"I'd like to stay and listen. I'm only vaguely aware that I do it, and once the composition's complete, I forget the words."

"You stay, Rosie." Vince gives me a crooked smile. "If Wes gets a chance to say 'hi' to Raelynn, maybe we won't have an uptight asshole for a producer on set."

"Don't call me Rosie. Please." I feel a crimson flush spread across my face.

"Ahh, it's a nickname, isn't it? For when your skin turns that beet-red color? Like right now."

I sigh. "Do we really need to discuss middle school nicknames?" I ask.

"I'll tell you mine if you tell me how you got yours," Vince offers.

"I think we should just keep our secrets," I reply.

"I'll let you buy me beer sometime, and maybe then we'll share," Vince says.

"You're leaving, right?" Wes asks.

Vince laughs before he bangs out an extended version of 'ta da' on his drums. Then he stands and places his sticks on the drum stool.

"See ya," he says, then exits out the glass door on the lower level by the pool. The outside lights illuminate the path to the stone staircase that leads up to the driveway. As he disappears into the darkness, I wonder if his harassment is some weird expression of friendship. I hope so.

When I turn back around, Jai's guitar case is slung over his shoulder.

"Sure you don't need a ride?" he asks me.

"I'm not a motorcycle kind of girl. Thanks though."

"If you ever change your mind, let me know. See you, guys."

Jai waves and takes the stairs to the upper level. Wes and I listen as his footsteps tread across the wood floor and out the front door, which slams behind him.

"Would you like another glass of wine?" Wes asks.

I swirl the almost empty contents of my glass. "Sounds good."

"Sure thing. I'll get the bottle and cue up the replay." He smiles. An easy, relaxed expression that gives me the impression he's been waiting all night for this.

Me too.

My neck arches back into the plush leather sofa and I put my bare feet up on the matching stool. I'm in a strange state of relaxed awareness. It's a combination of the composition work, the wine, and Wes.

Even with my eyes closed, I'm tuned in to Wes's movements around me. The thump of the cork being removed from the wine bottle. The patter of his feet as he retreats into the recording studio. The creak of the leather sofa as he sinks down beside me. The *gluck, gluck, gluck* of the wine being poured.

"You ready?" he asks.

I open my eyes and he hands me my glass of wine.

"Yeah."

CHAPTER TWENTY-SIX

WES

*A*fter she takes the glass, I grab my phone from the table and find the app to start the replay. When the music starts, it captures all her attention. The alert look in her eyes, the up and down motion of her head in beat with the song we made together. The way she blinks when she approves of something, the frown that appears when she doesn't.

Over the speaker system, her dark, delicious, broken voice delivers a deep-throated slow-motion melody that fades away on a long last note.

"... Coming back, would be so much better,
If I were coming back to you."

Listening to Rose makes me understand how female fans react to my performances.

"Nice," I tell her softly, trying not to break the spell she's cast on me. On us.

"Needs some work." Her words brim with self-depreciation.

"You have… a unique voice."

"That's not fair," she laughs unhappily. "We all sound like chickens getting our necks rung compared to you."

"I don't mean it in a bad way. It's just I've never heard a voice quite like yours."

"Probably not," Rose answers, then reaches for my old acoustic next to her on the sofa.

She strums with a distant look that's become familiar. I watch those slender fingers strum the guitar cradled in her lap while she improvises the chords of another new song.

I can't imagine feeling any more turned on just by being in the same room.

"In formal settings, I'm a contralto, the rarest voice type for a female singer." Her tone is matter of fact, but her expression hardens, and she strums again.

"Have you considered voice lessons? They helped me. A lot."

"I took voice classes at university," she explains as the melody she plays turns somber. "My instructor said I'm a lyric contralto, with a two-octave range and a semitone. He also told me that my voice was damaged."

"How?" She's lived my worst nightmare, and it horrifies me.

"Even though I attended a fine arts high school, the choir director mistook me for a mezzo soprano." The tempo of her somber melody quickens. "I injured myself trying to sing higher than my natural range. It was supposed to develop my voice. Instead, I hurt myself. Very, very badly."

"I'm so sorry." Wordlessly, I stroke her hair.

"It's no one's fault." Rose shudders at my touch. "Just bad luck. My college instructor told me that in his twenty years as a voice coach, I was only the third true contralto he'd trained."

"It's an occupational hazard. Bad training, poor technique, and overuse can damage us."

"No shit," she replies, weeping.

Tears stream down those porcelain cheeks, but she doesn't hide or turn away. I wipe a single streak with the pad of my thumb.

"Growing up, I played guitar in the school band but never took singing lessons. I was a natural, and there were only so many hours in the day. Chalk it up to youthful stupidity and arrogance.

"In my late teens and early twenties, I belted out three albums and two world tours. By twenty-six, the damage became obvious. Did my best to cover it up, changed my vocal style a bit, but without my voice coach… I probably wouldn't be singing today. And there's no way in hell I'd sound like Wes Anders."

"You've got an incredible gift. Saving it was the right thing to do. But my natural voice is dark, deep, and now raspy, which is so-not-the-norm."

"So-not-the-norm can be a good thing." I deliver a quick kiss. "You got my attention."

"Glad some good came out of it." She squeezes my arm. "But modern female singers are overwhelmingly sopranos. Many can even hit the whistle register. Even if my voice came back, it's not in demand."

"I don't know about that. Cher's a contralto. So is Tracy Chapman. Amy Winehouse was, too."

"Cher and Tracy are two of the most underrated vocalists. Ever. Amy's vocal range was far more expansive than mine, and she died before thirty. It's all good. My true passion was always musical composition and arrangements. The voice and instruments are just tools. I made my peace with that long ago."

"You tend to overthink things, don't you?"

"Not lately." She wipes her own tears away and snuggles under my arm. "I've... never told anyone this before, let alone cried about it in front of someone. But thank you for listening."

"Anytime. For real."

Rose lays the guitar against the side of the couch and curls into a ball beside me. Wisps of hair flutter against my nose and cheeks, inundating me with an intoxicating perfume that arouses and haunts me. The too familiar scents of vanilla and honeysuckle evoke emotions and memories that are familiar, befuddling, and wrong.

Not *wrong*, I tell myself. *Rose.*

I press my lips to that gorgeous mouth, kissing her with all the eager, pent up recklessness and frustration that consumes me whenever we're close. If my kiss provides a release for my primal need, it divulges her desire. Rose's lips are eager, soft, and responsive. She moans softly and arches her body gently into mine.

"Wes," she moans.

My hands slide down the firm planes of her body to

explore her breasts, stomach, and waist. She's wearing a long straight skirt with a slit that reaches the top of her thigh. I burrow my fingers under the hem and slide them up her leg, where they toy with a slim band of silk that rests high on the smooth skin of hip.

"Wes, please. Wait."

Wait. What? Whoa!

"Sorry." I push back from her to the far side of the couch. "I never meant to make you feel uncomfortable."

"Maybe that's just how I am around you." She breaks eye contact and looks down.

Fuck. It's because of her sister, I know it. I've tried to reassure her without going graphic, but it's gotten us nothing but guilt and frustration. Neither of which I do well.

"Okay, we need to settle this right now."

"Settle what?"

"It started with one kiss." I spit out. "Raelynn kissed me."

I stand up and pace in front of her. "We'd done lots of professional appearances as a 'couple.' We've kissed at photo calls dozens of times, but that night…"

"What about it?" Her eyes widen with alarm.

"After months of flirting and bring her flowers and asking her out, she kissed me for real."

Rose's jawline quivers. "I never knew all this happened before that night. I'm so sorry."

"Well… I probably deserved it." He gives me an ironic smile. "I won't lie. I've slept with women who liked me more than I liked them. Never led anyone on, but I didn't stop them from thinking whatever they wanted."

He nods to himself. "Like they say, what comes around goes around."

"You think… she used you? Like, sexually?" Rose sounds horrified.

"Hell yeah, she did. Raelynn knew I wanted more than a work relationship, and I make one helluva a bedpost notch. I am a rock star. But I'm over it, Rose, I swear. Please give me a chance to show you."

"Holy Shit," she moans as she covers her mouth with her hands. "The harder I try to make things easier, the more difficult they become." She retreats to her side of the couch. "I thought working on this video would make life easier for everyone. Turns out I didn't factor myself into that equation. Or you."

"I knew you liked me. For real." I tell her with gentle smugness.

"Of course I like you," she admits. "You're talented and creative and…"

"No. Hell no. You don't like me for that. You like me for this." I kneel between her legs and grip her hips, pulling her off the couch and up against my hard, rigid body.

"Damn it, Wes. Please." Her muffled groans drag her lips across the base of my throat.

My hands push her skirt sideways then up before they find the tender spot where the back of her thigh joins that delicious split-peach bottom. My fingers linger on her moist, tender folds and she cries out while arching into me.

"Like this," I repeat, my words coming in gasps.

"Like this," she admits as those pretty, pouty lips collide with the base of my throat.

They don't move but her soft breath arouses me even more. Damn it, I need her to know she does this to me. Her and no one else. I hoist her up into the air, and she coils those long legs tight around me. I carry her that way up the stairs to my bedroom.

CHAPTER TWENTY-SEVEN

ROSE

*M*y back rests against the wood of a smoothly polished door while Wes works the knob and then kicks it open.

The room is dark. From the paint on the walls to the mahogany leather chair and the masculine, dark-gray tones of the comforter on his king-sized bed. Th only brightness comes from the glow of the outside floodlights peeking in behind the drapes.

Wes sets me down at the foot of his bed, my arms still around his neck. From between my legs, he attacks the drawstring waist of my skirt, his strong fingers working the knot with hurried, deliberate motions. The force of him pulling the skirt down around my ankles puts me flat on my back.

"Slide up," he urges, then settles between my legs. I raise my hips and scoot backward, heels digging into the edge of the mattress.

"Take this off." He gives the hem of my tee-shirt an impatient tug.

Propping myself up on my elbows, I alternate between arms as he pulls the thin cotton fabric over my head, then tosses it over his shoulder. When his gaze shifts to me, he makes a sound that's somewhere between exhaling loudly and a whistle.

"Nice. Very nice. Did you wear this for me?"

It takes a moment and glance downward to grasp what he's seeing. I'm wearing a high-end luxury brand lingerie set in soft pearl gray. I bought it years ago when it was sold as a sample. It didn't fit back then, but it was so pretty I couldn't help myself. Since I slimmed down for the body double gig, it's perfect now.

At least while it lasts.

Wes was on my mind when I dressed today. This lingerie makes me feel sexy and confident, exactly what I needed in case *this* happened. But something holds me back from admitting it.

"Can't a woman wear pretty things just because?" I ask.

"Hell yeah." The back of his hand strokes the delicate lace of the silk demi-cut bra. "Lucky me," he murmurs, sitting back on his heels between my legs, watching me.

Wes breaks contact to finger the buttons of his black checkered shirt. When the top three buttons are open, he yanks the collar from behind his neck and pulls it off overhead.

Oh my God.

The familiar planes of his torso make the perfect canvas for ink splayed across his naked chest. When we were… together before, it felt intrusive to explore the elaborate tattoos that adorned his body.

It doesn't feel that way now.

Inked onto the left side of his chest is the simple line profile of a jester. A large heart, close to Wes's, encircles the eye of the tattooed figure.

"N-nice." Wes shivers as he watches me sit up and kiss the contrite mouth of the fool etched above his heart. He stands up on his knees, creating space to unfasten his pants as he kisses my neck below the ear.

His jeans and underwear come off in a single fluid motion before he kicks them off the bed behind him. Naked, Wes kneels in front of me, his body taut, aroused, and quivering.

"See something you like?" he asks.

I smile and nod, speechless.

"Good." He rubs the pad of his thumb against the tip of my protruding nipple through the filmy see-through fabric of my bra. Though his touch is incredibly gentle, my nipple hardens almost painfully.

I suck in an audible, hard breath.

While one hand teases my nipple, the other slides around the band of my bra and finds the closure. Single-handed, he unfastens the hook and eye. Once again, his uncanny knowledge of women's lingerie both impresses and disquiets me.

"I've tried so hard to stay away from you, Rose. I

can't do it anymore," he murmurs, sliding my bra off and tossing it away.

"Then don't," I whisper.

We've both tried keeping our distance, staying professional, and focusing on the work that needed to be done. It's been an epic fail. Every time we get close, things start off tentative then move to tender, until we're both overcome with a primal, feral heat.

Every time it happens, I fend off the thought that the reason we're like this around each other is because, deep down, deep, deep down, I know this can't and won't last.

And my biggest fear is that Wes knows it too.

Hard and hungry, his mouth descends on mine. I return the kiss with equal ferocity, as my familiar feral need for him takes over. My fingers lace behind his neck, pulling him against me as I fall back onto the pillow.

Those wicked lips descend lower and lower until they reach the waist of my panties. His tongue disappears underneath the elastic band, taunting my tender flesh as he wends to my hip. When he nibbles the bone, my pelvis makes uncontrolled thrusts.

He steadies me with a firm grip as he reaches inside the drawer of the bedside table.

"It's time for these to come off." He snaps the elastic waist of my Brazilian panties.

"Help me." I rub my hip against his as he rolls on a condom.

He laughs and gives my hip a playful slap as he slides my panties down. It catches me by surprise in more ways than one. It stings more than it hurts, elicits a half-groan, half gasp from me as a new sensation heightens my aroused state.

"Is that okay?" he asks, caressing me. "Some people find it enhances other sensations. In others it can ruin the mood."

"My mood's not ruined. How did you know?" I ask.

"Because I know you," he answers. "Maybe better than we both realized. That's a good thing."

"Why's that?"

"Let me show you. Trust me?"

I nod, and my knees leave the mattress one at a time as he drags the lacey undergarments down past my ankles and tosses them into the darkness.

When they're gone, he places his bent knees on the bed and walks toward the center until our torsos touch. I expect him to press me back into the mattress and straddle me. Instead, those powerful, dexterous hands grab the back of my upper thighs and hoist me onto his lap. His massive erection rubs against my strip of pubic hair.

My front smashes into his, and I feel the rapid beating of his heart against my chest. Wes kisses me, exploring my mouth and biting my lips gently. His hands reach under each of my upper thighs and urges me up and onto to his hard length.

I lean back and brace myself against the headboard as he inches forward into me. Once the broad tip passes my entrance, he surges forward with an eager, inpatient plunge. Our eyes meet and lock as we watch each other with fixated gazes as he strokes in and out of me. Slowly, he stretches and reaches deep. One of his hands grips the top of my thigh, while the other squeezes and teases my hard nipple.

The back of my legs rest along the tops of his thighs, my heels dug deep into the bed as we push and pull each other along our sensual pathway. Soon, a familiar tightening knots my core before it unfurls in a rush of intimate pulses.

"That's right, Rose," Wes urges me on. "Come. Come for us."

I couldn't stop if I tried. My heels crunch into the mattress as my back arches into the air. Wes pushes forward, and as I reach my perfect peak, his hands sting my naked rump at just the… right moment.

I can't speak. Or think. All I can do is revel in the intensity of an already potent experience.

"That's right, Rose. Enjoy it. Enjoy me," he utters with breathless efforts before he explodes, bracing himself with arms braced against the headboard.

As he falls on top of me, I take strange comfort in hearing him cry out my name.

"Rosalie, God, yes, Rosalie."

CHAPTER TWENTY-EIGHT

ROSE

Maybe. Just… maybe things will be okay.

Beside me, Wes shifts in the king-sized bed. His hand trails along my back before he turns over and tucks me underneath his chin. The silky gray sheet becomes intertwined between his thighs, exposing the nude masculinity of his muscular back and legs.

In the morning light, his hairless skin possesses a pearly, luminescent quality that makes me sigh and wince at the same time. I want to stay here with him all day. Admittedly, I admired him from afar after he kept texting me, but up close and personal… nothing's changed.

Nothing, except that I like him even more than I expected.

In a business where people aren't always what they

seem, where teams of experts exist to project a perfect image, it's easy to be disappointed. Part of me assumed that's what would happen between us. Either Wes would find me unremarkable, or I'd discover real flaws behind his carefully cultivated image.

I don't know what's in his heart, but I know what's in mine.

Maybe this *can* work.

The intrusive lilt of an-all too familiar text tone destroys my morning after bliss. My first inclination is to ignore it, but I know from experience that will only result in persistent phone calls. As it stands, she's doubled, now triple texted me in the last few minutes.

Slowly, I slide my naked body from beneath the covers and search for my skirt. Thankfully, it landed close to the bed when Wes carried me in here. I pull the noisy cell phone from the hip pocket and open the text app.

RAELYNN: You're not home.
RAELYNN: Did u come home last night?
RAELYNN: Are you okay?
ME: Fine.
RAELYNN: R U coming home? I need to work

I don't want to see her right now. I don't want to help her get ready.

ME: I don't have a car. I can't promise what time I'll be home.
RAELYNN: I can send someone to get you. Huey will be here soon. Give me an address.

ME: I'll get back to you.

Before she can respond, I shut my phone off.

As if fate were trying to make my life harder, Wes stirs and flips onto his back. His masculine features combined with the contrast of black lashes and rose-pink against pearl-white skin and the gentle child-like curl of his mouth in slumber create a mass of contradictions that well up inside me as the urge to kiss him spikes then dies inside of me.

I roll out of bed and head for the shower.

"Good morning," a smokey angel's voice says. "Is there room for me in here?"

"Yeah, sure," I reply.

The shower door slides open and Wes leans his muscular, toned body against the tile wall and smiles at me. On any other day, he would be irresistible. Today's not that day.

"Um, I have… things to do." I step aside to make room for him. As I try to escape through the sliding door, Wes takes my hand in his. "Work things."

He nods, understanding what I mean without saying her name. "Stay with me. Let me wash your back."

"That's nice. But…"

Wes pulls me back inside, one hand massages my shoulder while the other pumps out light herbal body wash from a dispenser. His touch mesmerizes me.

"I, I need to get dressed and call an Uber."

"Relax, Rose. It's still early, and I can take you home," he replies, massaging the shower gel onto my back.

Damn, that's heaven.

"Are you sure?"

"No problem. I've got to go into the studio anyway."

"On a Saturday?"

"Yeah. There's no filming today, but there's plenty of footage to go over and stuff to tweak."

"Right," I answer, just as he steers me into the shower jet by my ticklish hip and rinses away the gel. My god, it's hard to concentrate.

"You know, I was thinking... you've got work, I've got work, the entire day's shot before we get started." He turns toward the shower jet and plunges his face into the fast-moving stream of water, where he lingers. I could stay all day, but the more I linger, the harder it is to leave. As I slide the shower door open, he pulls his face out of the water stream.

"Why don't you come back here tonight?" he asks.

"That sounds nice, but—"

"No buts. Just come back. I enjoy having you around."

"Thanks. I like you, too. But wouldn't it be easier to wait until the video wrapped?"

"It wraps this week. What's the difference?"

"Life is going in a million different directions for us right now. I just thought if things were less hectic, we could take our time?"

Wes's body stiffens. He puts his forearm up against the shower wall and gives me an assessing look. Then he pumps shampoo in his hands and rubs it through his hair.

For a few endless moments, the only sound is the shower spray.

Ouch.

Maybe he doesn't need time. Maybe this is a fast and furious fling for him. Fine. Better I know now.

"I wasn't planning to make an announcement." Wes tilts his head out of the stream to speak. "But I don't intend to act like we're strangers either. Besides, only the guys know, and we never spread each other's business around like that."

"The guys. And probably Nikki, who dropped me off last night. Then there's my sister, soon enough." My fingers wring my hair dry, a half-nervous, half-practical gesture. I need time to process all of this.

"I don't see what difference another few days will make." From beneath the watery veil, he flashes me a perfect smile. "But if you need to sort things out, I understand. Just… think about coming back tonight?"

Stunned by his request, I step out of the shower and reach for a plush, pure-white towel. I take my time, scrubbing my hair and body vigorously before wrapping the towel around my chest with a firm tuck.

"We can have dinner." He gives me a reserved but wicked smile. "Listen to the recordings we never finished. Go for a swim? I have a nice pool that hasn't been used in ages. You'd be doing me a huge favor."

The image of me doing Wes a favor by swimming in his pool makes me laugh out loud.

"You're a big girl, and we're sure as hell not doing anything wrong. If anyone asks where you went, lie. That's what I do."

"You're good with lying?"

"If someone's being a pain in my ass over something that's not their business? Yeah, I might."

When I turn to face him, he's standing beside me on the shower matt, his body dripping and naked.

"And what if things end up back here?" I gesture between our bodies.

"I'm good with that. Or not." His intense expression bores into me. "Just think about it. Please?"

"I'll think about it," I answer, against my better judgment. When it comes to Wes, my self-control doesn't exist.

"Good."

As I turn to leave, he gives my rear a firm, playful slap.

CHAPTER TWENTY-NINE

ROSE

"*R*osalie! I know that's you," Raelynn calls from the upstairs hallway seconds after the front door slams shut.

The *click-click* of my chunky sandals on the tile staircase gives away my location, and by the time I've climbed the stairs Raelynn is standing in front of me.

"Did you forget I had an appearance today?" she asks, hands on her hips.

"Isn't Nikki here? She's your assistant until I'm done with the video." I look outside through the large atrium window at the white hybrid sandwiched between several other familiar vehicles. "The car's here."

"I told her—" Raelynn gasps and I know she's not looking at the hybrid.

She's watching Wes's convertible pull out of the driveway.

"Rose, were you with… *him* last night?" Her voice is low with practiced caution. We're not alone this morning. Others are here to help her get ready.

"Maybe," I reply.

She looks me up and down, her eyebrows raising as she recognizes my clothes from yesterday. "Come to my room. Nothing you own fits anymore. Let's find you something to wear."

Experience makes me hesitate. It's clear she wants to speak with me in private. Although we've always been close, lately she's always in boss mode during our conversations.

I'm not willing to be 'bossed' about last night.

It's one of the many reasons being her assistant has started to suck. As Raelynn turns and walks toward her bedroom, she assumes I'll follow. Instead, I prop my elbow onto the banister and cup my chin.

When she reaches her door and realizes I haven't budged, she looks back at me and glares. "Give me ten minutes, Rose. Come on. I really do have to work today."

"Is Coraline up here?" I had noticed her car outside next to the hybrid "Because I'm not interested in her two cents on a good day."

"She's with Jason downstairs having coffee. It's just us. Sisters. Please?"

With wary reluctance, I approach her bedroom door. After we're both inside Raelynn closes it with a firm thud.

"You and Wes Anders? When did this happen?" She looks… horrified.

"About twelve hours a go," I reply.

"Twelve? You've only been working on the video for a week. I can't believe you slept with him so fast. That's not like you."

I want to tell her about the texts that went on for months but defending myself that way will cause far more problems than it solves. Instead, I collapse onto her bed and tuck my knees under my chin, gently rocking myself.

"Rae, I reserve the right to mind my own business."

"What?"

"I don't want to discuss this with you, okay?"

"It's not that simple," she tells me.

"For me it is," I reply.

"Rose, I don't think you and Wes together is a good idea."

I lower myself back on the bed beside her and stare at the ceiling. "Why?"

"Well, for starters, he doesn't have a great reputation."

"What rock star does?"

"Rose, I don't get my information from Twitter," she warns.

"Wherever you've sourced it from, it sounds out-of-date. If anything, he reminds me of you." I turn on my side to watch her. "Career first, everyone and everything else second," I reply.

"That's not fair." She folds her arms. "My job is not nine-to-five. You know that. And I'm working on the personal side of things, too,"

"Not with me you aren't." I sit up again. "Is that your problem with Wes? Not his rocker rep or his conversations you find a total bore." I swallow hard. "Maybe he's just someone who competes for my time, which you take for granted."

"I do not!" she shouts at me before her eyes dart to the closed door. "I do not," she repeats in a harsh whisper.

"Nikki is your assistant while I'm working on the video. Why isn't she here?"

"You're much more experienced than Nikki. I told her you had it covered," Raelynn gives a dismissive shrug.

"You mean you assumed I'd be around and wouldn't mind arranging my day off to suit you." My measured tone surprises me.

Her response is far less subdued.

"You live here, in my house. I pay you a good salary." She waves up and down at my wrinkled outfit from yesterday. "I even supplement your wardrobe. Speaking of which, I need to find you some clothes. You're a hot mess."

She disappears into her massive walk-in closet and rustles around inside, leaving me alone, frustrated, and drained. As twins, it's hellish for both of us when we argue.

When Raelynn's upset, I compensate by doing more for her, both at home and work. It's my way of assuring her I'm here for her when communication is not a thing.

If I'm the one who's upset, Raelynn gifts me things. Like now. Listening to hangers screech with agitated movement as she assaults her clothes closet. The last thing I need right now is a new designer wardrobe.

What I need is for my sister to listen.

"Try these." Raelynn emerges with a dozen articles of clothing and drops them on the bed next to me. "It's fun to share clothes, and we haven't done it in a long time."

For a split second, I wonder if that's a dig at my weight, another of my many flaws that irritate her. Then it occurs to me that even if it is, I no longer give a damn.

"Rae, I don't want any clothes." My raised voice stuns her and she drops a shirt she'd held up to me onto the bed. "I want to know why you didn't tell me that Wes Anders expressed genuine interest and asked you out."

Her expression confirms my suspicions.

"It wasn't important. I didn't think it mattered," she says. "He's got a reputation, or he did. I thought he was out to see what he could get."

"It mattered to me," I tell her. "I would've never pretended to be you if I'd known he liked you."

"Why the hell not?"

"Because that's a rotten thing to do someone." I feel tears well in my eyes. "I really like him. And it hurts to know that he liked you first, and that maybe I'm a close second."

"Just be careful," she warns me. "The video's done this week and it will settle all contractual obligations. Bide your time, see what happens."

"You're still worried he'll come after you for being a no-show at his launch party? That's your big concern here? Damn it, Raelynn, I'm not a sister, I'm an appendage." I pull away from her and head toward the door.

We stare at each other and communicate in perfect silence. She dislikes Wes, she doesn't want us dating, and she feels her career is more important than my feelings.

"I'm not coming back tonight," I tell her. "Get Nikki to help as much she can before school in the fall."

Raelynn's ready to go full-tilt diva on me when a loud knock on the door interrupts what I'm sure would be the nastiest fight we've had in years.

"Ready for makeup? Someone needs to watch the clock!" It's Jason, Raelynn's makeup artist.

"Raelynn's ready," I call to him. "One moment, I'll get the door."

Before she can protest, I pull open the door and give Jason my best sincere-fake smile. "Please come in!"

"Thank you, beautiful," he aims an air kiss at my cheek.

"It's nice to see you, too."

"Are you riding with Raelynn?" he asks. "I can give you a little glow before you go. You look tired today, darling."

"Thank you for the offer, but I have other plans." I smile at Jason, then turn to Raelynn and give her a curt, final nod.

"Oh." Jason's stunned murmur is the last thing I hear as I head down the hall toward my room.

CHAPTER THIRTY

WES

"*W*hat are you doing here?" I ask.

It's Saturday afternoon, and the last person I expected to run into at the studio was Vince. He's alone in the editing room, and from the looks of the surrounding computer screens, he's checking the overlay sound from our video.

Vince's head nods back at me without looking up. "Thought you'd be busy this weekend, and someone needed to mind the store."

"I didn't realize you gave a fuck about this back-end stuff."

Vince swivels the chair around and faces me. "I don't. Unless I'm afraid shit is going sideways. Then I give tremendous fucks."

"It's not." I give a dismissive wave.

"Really?" Vince's jawline tightens. "You're banging two sisters who the band is incredibly dependent on right now. And after meeting Rose, this doesn't seem like a wet and wild adventure, at least for her. Do you have a plan for when this goes nuclear?"

Fuck.

I'd agreed to keep things with Rose quiet until the video was over. But it's Vince's livelihood too, and he's got a right to know what's going on. I grab the office chair next to another workstation and wheel it alongside Vince.

"Raelynn and I parted ways a while ago. There's no issue." My voice projects more confidence than I feel.

Vince laughs out loud. That hyper-masculine, alpha-esque asshole laugh that sets me on edge. "I guess not. Unless you're planning on trying to stay with Rose."

"What the hell does that mean?"

"It means she's a keeper, and if you don't want her, then let her go, because she's not the type who plays like that." Vince gives me a pointed look that brings my blood to a boil.

"You?" I'm angry and shocked. "Does this mean you're on to Rose and over Avery?"

"I never got over Avery. I never will." Vince's expression softens to resigned. "But a man reaches a point in life where he understands the benefits of waking up with a good woman beside him every day. I'm there, and you're...?" He throws his hands in the air.

"I'm... working it out," I admit.

"Let me guess what you're working out." Vince leads

forward in his office chair. "How's the sex? Start with whoever you want."

"Fuck off," I tell him, standing up. "I'm not going there."

"You will, you have, and you are," he replies.

Vince stands up too. For a minute I think we're going to square off and I put my fists up. Vince looks at my arms, shakes his head, then walks to the office door and shuts it with a quiet thud.

"I never cheated on Avery." Vince leans his back against the door, arms folded. "I know what everyone said, but that's the truth. We took a break from each other, and, uh, I hooked up with someone else. A close friend of hers."

"Mia?" I think that was her name.

"Yeah," he confirms. "They'd known each other in high school. They were close. She's no Avery, but there was chemistry, and I was the asshole rock star. Who would blame me?" Vince blows out an uneasy breath.

"Let me guess," I say. "Avery?"

Vince responds with a silent thumbs up and a sad nod. "Avery was super-pissed when she found out. At first, we tried to be adults about it, accept what happened and move on. What a load of naïve bullshit."

"Avery broke up with you?" Vince hadn't offered details at the time.

"More like she gave me a hard pass when I got my shit together and realized I loved her." Vince stares at the carpet and nods to himself. "The truth is, if they hadn't been so close, I think Avery could've forgiven me."

"Whatever happened to her? One day she just stopped being around," I recall.

"Sometimes it's over just like that," Vince says. "She married a cardiologist. Not as fun or flashy as we are. Or as rich. But he makes enough, and he treats her like a queen. I can't compete with that, and I sure as fuck can't undo what I've done. And you can't either."

A strange, silent understanding passes between us. Vince can be an asshole, but he's not being one now. He's trying to keep me from being burned like he was and taking the band down in flames with me.

"I wish I'd never slept with Raelynn Tailor." My admission shatters the silence between us.

"That good or that bad?" Vince asks.

"Both."

"Oh… fuck." Vince says.

"Our night at HotZone… I'll never ever forget." It unnerves me that I'm saying these things out loud. "She was playful, passionate, raw, and real. We both fucked like it was going to be our last time. I guess it was. It was the best time I've ever had. Until Rosalie."

"It's worse than I thought," Vince mumbles.

"Yeah, I know. Rose is every bit into it when she commits, like her sister. It's fucking unnerving how alike they are in that way. I've been trying to cope with it since last night."

"Tell the truth. Do you think you'd ever be tempted to sleep with Raelynn again?"

"Never." My palms sweat. "Because I know it would cost me Rose. She's every bit as passionate as her sister, and she's so much more… we connect in ways that are new to me. I feel like I've known her much longer than I actually have."

"Are you in love with her?" Vince asks.

I rub my sticky palms up against my denim covered thighs. "It's possible. Maybe... yeah."

"Yeah?"

"Yeah."

"Then you need to go make peace with her sister."

"We have, sort of," I say. "She doesn't want to talk to me, and I stopped trying a while ago."

"That sounds like a truce, not peace." Vince becomes quiet for a moment. "Is she freezing you out or did you piss her off?"

Images of my abrupt, naked departure from the private VIP lounge at HotZone flood my memories. "I might've pissed her off."

"You sure love a challenge, don't you, Wes?" Vince blows out a breath. "My relationship with Mia fizzled out fast. I knew right away that it was a mistake, and it made me realize how much I loved Avery. But Mia was hurt, and they were still friends. She confided in Avery, whose anger was only compounded by her friend's pain," he reveals.

"I'm lucky that way, I guess. Rose knows what happened between me and her sister."

"But does Raelynn know what happened between you and Rose?" he asks.

"If she doesn't, she will. They tell each other everything," I say.

Vince jumps away from the door, his arms outstretched, and exclaims, "How can you not see that's a problem, especially if Raelynn trash talks you to Rose?"

Alarm courses through my body like a jolt of electricity. "Oh fuck. I've done everything to make amends, and even then, she told me to get lost. She's got no reason trash talk me."

"If she believes you'll mistreat Rose, she does."

"I would never do that. Not fucking ever."

"Then tell Raelynn. Explain your feelings for Rose, how important she is to you, and that you want to move on from what happened."

"Anything else?"

"Then tell Rose you spoke to her sister."

I nod in agreement. Rose needs to know it's her I want, and only her. Part of me can't believe I'm taking relationship advice from Vince, of all people, but my guts tells me he's right. Or at least, less wrong than me.

My phone buzzes. It's Rose.

"Speak of the she-devil…" Vince teases.

ROSE: Got plans tonight?
ME: Not yet.
ROSE: I'd like to go for a swim, if the offer's still open.
ME: My place at eight.
ROSE: See you there

After I'm done, I glance at the phone's clock. It's two-thirty. Five and a half hours before I can see Rose. The thought of puttering around the house all day alone waiting for her to arrive makes me feel more whipped than I'm ready to admit.

Besides, being at the studio was what I planned on doing anyway.

"Hey, Vince, need a hand with that overlay?"

CHAPTER THIRTY-ONE

ROSE

*W*es lies beside me on the plush couch, left leg flung over my hip, his chin resting on the top of my head. He's out cold, his breathing heavy, even, and deep.

Wish that I could say the same.

After my blowout with Raelynn, I courageously hid in my room until her entourage got her ready and she left for her appearance. It felt like an episode of delayed adolescence. Hiding in my room until everyone left? Really?

The upside was it gave me time to select some outfits for my visit to Wes, a rare occurrence for me. It's like how top chefs often say they eat cereal for their dinner because they're too tired to cook for themselves after a long shift.

When you're an assistant who spends hours tracking

down the perfect accessories or enduring debates about the correct shade of lipstick, your wardrobe choices tend toward comfortable, clean, and practical in no particular order.

My eyes blink hard at the memory of the clown ensemble I wore when Wes and I met in person the first time. That wasn't happening again. Not tonight, not ever.

After some deliberations, I chose a revealing black monokini, with a white crocheted cover up. I barely made it inside the house before he had me flat on my back.

My… relationship with Wes leaves me traversing the extremes between elation, exhaustion, and insomnia. Motivated by creativity and passion, there's a quiet intensity that surrounds his private life and the things that matter. Wes pursues financial success so he can continue to make music, not the other way around.

I'm okay with that. I mean the part about the fame and adulation being a by-product of the job and not the main pursuit. But he's also driven and determined to get what he wants, and I already live with someone like that.

Wes and Rae are A-listers in their respective industries. Wasn't that how they met? Some marketing mastermind thought a rock star-model couple would be popular with the public and paying customers alike? Look how right they were…

Maybe that's why I haven't worked up the nerve to tell him the truth about what happened at his launch party. He'd obviously feel deceived, and there's nothing to be done about that. But there's no way to convince him my feelings were genuine unless I tell him about the texts from Raelynn's number.

It's odd, but I'm even more ashamed about the texts than I am about the sex. One lie leads to another, but a single truth can shatter many lies at once. You can't tell the truth incrementally the way you can lie. I need to tell him everything. I just can't figure out where to start.

"Oof," Wes mumbles as I raise my head from the pillow and knock into his chin. He turns onto his opposite side and curling outward pushes me to the edge of the couch.

That's okay, I want to get up anyway.

Resisting the urge to spoon him, I roll my naked body off the edge of the couch and hit the floor with a gentle thud. My crocheted cover-up lies between the coffee table and plush couch. I pull it over my body before contemplating what to do next.

Grogginess hits me square between the eyes as I try to focus on the black hands of the clock. It's three-thirty. The last thing I want is to wake him, but it doesn't feel right wandering around his house in the dark either.

Through the large glass patio doors, I notice underwater lights illuminating the bluish water of the zero-edge pool. Wes must have turned them on earlier, then forgot after our sudden change of plans.

After a quick glance at Wes's soundly sleeping form, I smile into the welcoming darkness. Now seems like the perfect time for that swim he promised me. Wes startles at the sharp click of the deadbolt as my fingers twist it open, but then he settles back into a deep sleep.

It's perfect right now. The days have been long and hot, heating the pool water to a pleasant lukewarm temperature, while the pre-dawn air holds a cool freshness.

Since I don't know where my swimsuit landed, and unexpected company is unlikely at this hour, I strip back down to nothing as I stand at the welcoming edge of the pool. I take a deep breath, then enter the pool with an almost splashless dive.

My head rests against the edge of a cement step as I drift in and out of sleep. A loud whoosh sound brings me out of my semi-conscious state in time to see Wes emerge from the sliding glass door.

"How you doing?" he calls to me. "It gets cold out here you know."

He's wearing a long, super plush cotton terry robe and hugs a thick stack of fluffy towels under one arm. He carries a steel carafe that I hope holds coffee, and an unopened carton of cream is tucked under his chin as he walks to the patio table.

"It sure does," I agree, turning on my side to face him. "Did I wake you?"

"Nope. Turned over and you weren't there. Waited for you to come back. When you didn't, I came to find you."

I did wake him. Shit.

"Sorry."

"Don't worry about it. The couch isn't comfortable enough for two people. It's my fault, I should've been a better a host." He tilts his head and gives me a crooked smile. "Are you coming out or am I coming in?"

"Get me out of here." I start to stand but re-submerge myself. "Uh, Wes?"

"Yeah?"

"I'm naked."

"You sure are. Watched you swimming from the kitchen window while the coffee brewed. Nice."

Our eyes meet and mine roll at him. "I couldn't find my swimsuit and didn't want to wake you."

"Does that mean you're not trying to turn me on?" He sounds disappointed.

"Not right now… maybe later."

"Too late." He gives me an impish smile. "But since your lips are such a pretty shade of blue, I forgive you. Just once though."

He takes a white towel off the table, walks to the edge of the pool, and unfurls it for me.

"Tha-a-nks," I reply between shivering teeth. I stand and wrap myself in the waiting towel. When he feels my hands, he opens his eyes and wraps it around me, then rubs my back down to dry me off.

"Come on." He steers me to the table. "There's another towel for your hair."

Wes pulls the chair out for me. When I'm seated, he hands me the other towel and reaches for the carafe and a large white mug.

"Coffee?" he offers me after I secure the second towel around my head.

"God, yes. Please" I take the steamy mug from him gratefully. "Isn't it too early though?"

"I can't sleep now," he says. "Might as well start the day early."

I respond with a silent nod and savor the warmth of my coffee.

We sit in silence and adjust to each other's presence. Early mornings aren't my style, and it's got to be almost five. After several large sips of coffee, I'm alert enough to notice Wes watching me.

Billows of steam float from his coffee cup that sits untouched. One hand cups his elbow, the other grips his chin. Those long legs peek out from the thick terry cotton robe. His feet are crossed at the ankles underneath my chair.

When I give him a questioning look, he taps his heel rapidly.

"Is... something wrong?" I ask.

"No. Uh, nope." He grabs his coffee. "Oh, um, your swimsuit landed on Vince's snare drum. Remember to take it. Otherwise, he'll think it's a present."

"We can't have that," I agree. "Don't worry, I'll find it."

"Good. That's good." He picks up his coffee cup and it sloshes over the brim onto the plush sleeve cuff of his robe. He mutters, then sets it back on the table. "So... only a few more days before the video wraps."

"Homestretch now." My sigh is louder than I intended. "Can't wait."

"Why? Are you unhappy working with us?"

"Not at all. It's been great. I'm just excited to see the finished product."

"Oh. Right." Wes visibly bounces in his chair. "Did you find another job?"

"Not yet." It's tough to admit. "But I've reached out to

a friend from my TV show days and let him know I'm looking for work. My friend, Brad, invited me to lunch next week. Hopefully, he's got good news."

"Brad?" he repeats with a slight edge.

"There were five assistant composers where I worked, including the interns. Brad was one of them. He was more experienced. When the show tanked, he found another job right away."

"How would you feel... about working for us?" He says the words slowly.

"Us?"

"Me and the guys."

My response is stunned silence and a blank look.

"Jester's Edge? Maybe you've heard of us?" his voice is a blend of nervous impatience.

"Wow." The hairs on my nape spike. "Thank you, but it's like I said before. I'm done being a PA. I need to get back to my real career, such as it is."

"Wait a sec." Wes rakes a hand through his thick black hair. "I love Felix. In a totally appropriate, heterosexual boss kind of way. I can't function without him and wouldn't dream of replacing him."

"You want... two PAs? Like another for the band?" I ask.

"Hell, no. I want to hire you to work on our songs." His expression softens. "We've written two fucking great songs together and tweaked the arrangement on another one and saved it from the scrap heap. You've got untapped potential as a lyricist that should be explored. You're amazing, Rose. Please say yes."

For a split second, my life flashes before me.

At first, it's a magical mixture of music. Composi-
tions. Arrangements. Lyrics. An impressive portfolio that
supplies both pride and future job security. Toss in plenty
of late nights and early mornings with Wes.

Then the darkness of uncertainty enters the picture.

Wes. Me. Rae. Jai. Vince. I've seen enough to know
that if things crash, it will be me who's out of a job and
career. Again.

"No." My voice is strained, tight, and barely audible.
"I can't."

Wes's expression is a mix of hurt and disbelief.

"Rose, this isn't an assistant's gig. We'll pay you fair-
ly and you'll get credit for your work. Jai and Vince both
like you and respect your talent."

Stress makes me want to tug at my hair, but the towel
gets in the way and falls to my shoulders. I wrap it around
my arms and speak with rapid bursts of thought and
energy.

"Wes. It's a wonderful offer." I reach over and touch
his wrist. He shifts until there's no flesh-to-flesh contact,
only thick layers of terrycloth.

At least he didn't pull entirely away.

"If I've learned anything from the last four years, it's
that I'm miserable working for someone with so much
influence over my personal and professional life. I get
steamrolled all the time. Being more successful than me
only makes it worse."

"You're refusing because of your sister?"

Damn. I know where this is going. If I say no, it's a
lie. If I say yes, it's unfair.

"Not the way you think. I want, no, need a chance to

keep my personal and professional life separate. I'm not driven like you are, and I'll cave in on something if I think it will damage our relationship, even if hurts my career. You won't. You're too ambitious."

Wes studies me with an enigmatic expression. Shocked, angry, disappointed, sad, they're all possibilities and I'm not about to ask. Right on cue, I feel tears well up, knowing I've disappointed him. Part of me wants to change my answer just to make him feel better. But I know where that leads.

"I should shower and get dressed." I stand and head toward the door, then stop behind his chair. "Thank you. Thank you for thinking I was good enough to work for you," I whisper from above, then plant a chaste kiss on the top of his head. "It means more than you know."

"You're welcome. Get dressed. I'll buy you breakfast."

CHAPTER THIRTY-TWO

WES

*S*he's late, damn it.

If Raelynn is a no-show, I'm going to camp out on her front porch until we talk.

The video wraps in a few days and Raelynn's due on set. I hoped that asking to meet up somewhere neutral would make her more likely to show.

Rose hasn't spent the night since Saturday. My mind keeps going over her reluctance to work for us. The connection with her sister. I know she didn't say that outright, but she didn't deny it either when I straight-up asked her. Now here I am, taking relationship advice from Vince of all people, and trying to smooth things over so everyone will relax about my relationship with Rose.

What a clusterfuck.

I'm peeling the chipped varnish off the table when Raelynn enters La Buena Vida, my favorite coffee shop, from the back entrance by the parking lot. I stand, pull the brim of my baseball cap down, and remove my dark sunglasses for a second.

"Thanks for meeting me." I stand and pull the chair out from the table occupying a secluded corner.

She doesn't speak, merely nods. It causes her over-sized straw hat with the pink brim to fan the air, obscuring my view of her eyes. She settles into the chair I offer and crosses her long denim-clad legs. Then her hips twist sideways, putting as much distance between herself, the table, and my seat across from her.

"Do you want something?" I nod toward the barista.

She gives me a calculating look. "Pomegranate iced tea."

I walk toward the counter to where my espresso waits and ask for a pomegranate tea. I'm well known here, and by the time I'm done adding low-cal sweetener to my cold-brewed espresso, Raelynn's drink is sitting next to mine.

I place the iced tea in front of her and she stiffens. "Thank you." Her tone is curt, clipped.

"Relax, Raelynn. Jesus." I sit down and study her face for the first time since she arrived.

Her hair is dyed a rich butter blonde, which makes those striking eyes pop. That pale gold skin is billboard flawless thanks to a layer of makeup that no doubt hides freckles like the ones scattered along the bridge of Rosalie's nose and cheeks.

The nude halter top slouches off her shoulder,

revealing the fit planes of toned arms and chest. She's thinner than Rosalie, but in a way that evokes concern rather than attraction.

At least now, anyway.

"I'm only here to talk about my sister."

"Good. Because she's all I want to talk about." I lean back on my wooden chair. "I've gotten to know Rose really well while we filmed the video. She's sweet, helpful, and kind."

"I know all this, Wes. Please get to the point."

All her inpatient hostility grates on my nerves. I take my dark glasses off slowly and spin them by one of the arms. I'm not trying to irritate her. I want to discuss what I came here for and not lose my temper.

"Rose is really special to me, and I want to continue having her in my life once the video ends." I reach out and let my fingertips brush her hand. "Because of our history, I felt like we should clear the air between us."

"History?" she's incredulous. "We don't have a history. We have a working relationship that ends in a few short days."

We stare at each other in silence. I'm not in the mood to appease her hostility, and veiled threats about work on the video won't calm me down.

Keep calm. Keep calm, I remind myself.

"I've apologized about what happened at HotZone. I'm not doing it again. The fact is, Raelynn, you're timing sucked."

"*My* timing?"

"Oh, just stop it." I look around and remind myself not

to speak too loudly. "Of all the nights you picked to come on to me, you chose the biggest night of my life."

Her blue eyes bulge in response, and she takes a quick sip of her tea. She clears her throat and looks around the coffee shop. It's two-thirty, so there aren't many people.

She whispers across the table. "I think there was a misunderstanding that night—"

"Misunderstanding? You kissed me. What did I misunderstand?"

"We, we, were at a photo call." She shifts in her chair and clanks the ice against the sides of the glass as she swirls her tea.

"Why do you act like I'm the last guy you'd ever sleep with? I'm a rock star. It happens."

"I'm sure it does." She brings the glass to her mouth again.

"It does, and it did. Were you just being a tease? Did you assume with everything going on that I'd be the one who'd put the brakes on having sex, and then you got pissed off when I didn't?"

A forceful spray of blood red tea erupts from Raelynn's lips, splattering across the pristine tabletop while droplets reach all the way to my white tee shirt. For a split second I'm shocked and super pissed because she's just spat on me, but when I look up at her face, it's pale, and her jaw is contorted like she's choking.

"Raelynn?"

Instead of answering, she waves a hand at me before striking her own chest with it.

"Everything okay?" the barista shouts from the counter.

Raelynn's eyes meet mine and they bulge with panic. Neither one of us wants a scene.

"Yeah, we're good." I try to look and sound casual.

I kneel beside Raelynn's bent torso and give the top of her back a firm strike. It seems to help. Raelynn gasps, then takes a huge gulp of air.

"Are you okay?" I ask, concerned.

She nods but still doesn't speak.

My eyes dart around the café. A few people who are seated nearby watch us with a mixture of concern and recognition. The barista approaches us but I raise my hand to stop him.

"Can you get us some napkins and a glass of room temperature water?"

He nods and turns back.

"Raelynn, say something," I insist.

"I'm okay." She sucks in a large gulp of air. "I swallowed a few ice cubes and they went down the wrong way."

"Take it easy."

She looks at the table, the glass in her lap, stained clothes, and the red dots across the chest of my tee-shirt.

"Holy shit." Her eyes widen in horror. "Wes, I'm so sorry. It was a complete accident, I swear."

"I know." I stand and walk toward the barista as he approaches with napkins and a water glass. "Thanks."

"Is she okay?" He nods at Raelynn.

"Fine. I'm fine," Raelynn calls from the table without turning around. "Thank you."

I hand her the napkins, set the water glass down, and give her a few minutes to collect herself. She removes the

glass from her lap and starts dabbing her jeans. After
throwing a mass of soaked paper napkins onto the table,
Raelynn pats her face and chest with another huge wad.
Through it all, she curses and sobs.

"What a disaster. I need to get out of here," she throws
a twenty on the trashed tabletop. "Can we go for a drive or
something?"

"My car's out back. I can take you home if you want."

"Perfect. Lead the way."

She stands and we move away from the table toward
the restrooms, which I know from experience leads to an
exit door. As Raelynn walks down the slender corridor, I
exchange a brief nod with the barista. Seconds later, I
catch up to where she waits and push the bar labeled
'emergency exit only.' An alarm sounds briefly, but when
it stops, we're long gone.

My Chevelle purrs loudly as I downshift into the curve on
the exit ramp from I-5. The convertible top is down, but
even with the windows up it's hard to talk. She hasn't said
a word yet and I've let it go. Rosalie's too important, and I
can't let Raelynn evade me forever.

"Rose loves you a lot," I say.

My words hang in the air between us for a few
moments as Raelynn processes them. The silence
stretches out so long I wonder if she heard me.

"What's that got to do with you?" Her tone is short
and clipped.

"I want her to be happy. Us to be happy, and she's

reluctant to explore the possibility because of my past history with you," I explain.

She folds her arms defensively. "I love Rose very much, but the idea of you two together is nothing short of god-awful."

"What the hell? Why would you say a thing like that?" My hands tighten their grip on the wheel.

"You're a rock star with a terrible reputation, for starters."

"Oh, hell, Raelynn. You know that's part of the job description." As we reach the local surface street, I'm grateful to focus on the road ahead. "Okay, I did some shit in my late teens and early twenties. Who hasn't? But that was ages ago. They only publish bad boy stories about me and you, and we both know those are nothing but ridiculous fiction."

"Rose is a sweet person, but she's not ambitious. She works for me, lives with me. I pay her a good salary. It works well for everyone."

Her perception of Rose startles me. I thought they were close, but she doesn't know Rose very well. The light at the corner changes to red, and I look over at her.

"Rose wants to work as a musician again."

"Oh, please. She lasted six months."

"They cancelled her show."

"She never found another job."

"Because you needed an assistant."

"You think I couldn't have found someone else?" She's dismissive.

"Someone else you could be sure wouldn't steal from you?" I ask.

Raelynn turns back to me and gasps.

"Help that won't rob us blind is rare and precious commodity. Yeah, I know about your last assistant.

That shuts her up, and I take advantage.

"Rosalie is a very talented musician. She's not weak or indecisive like you want to believe. Whether or not you admit it, Rosalie's done a lot for you too. Maybe it's time for you to honor her wishes instead of assuming you know what she wants. Or what's best for her."

We pull into the large circular driveway in front of her house. She smooths her clothes and adjusts her halter top. That's when I notice the tattoo that peaks out from the sleeve that slides down her shoulder.

It's a tiny butterfly, and I've never seen it before.

"Hold up." I touch the exposed butterfly. "When did you get this?"

She looks down at where my fingers brush her tanned flesh. "A few years ago. My first swimsuit issue. It's small enough to airbrush out if it's a problem. Why?"

The night we spent together I committed every inch of her perfect body to memory.

There was no tattoo. Anywhere.

Our eyes meet, and a flash of realization crosses her face. She tries to cover the tattoo and pull away from me. But before she can open the car door, I slide across the seat and kiss her. Hard and fast, like the last time at HotZone.

Only… nothing.

Not even a faint spark of the electric heat from our first encounter. Her beautiful lips feel over-plump and stiff, likely from recent fillers. The smell of vanilla, mint, and honeysuckle is absent, replaced by the scent of five-hundred dollar an ounce perfume. Chyre, I think. Her skin is silky smooth but cool and unresponsive.

I pull away, repelled by the unfamiliar.

"It wasn't you," I say with firm conviction. "That night at HotZone... that wasn't you. Which means there's only one other person it could be."

Rosalie.

"Wes, please," Raelynn tries to calm me. "I never meant for this to happen. I didn't know until now that you and Rosalie slept together at the launch. I still can't believe it." She looks dazed.

"You never meant? Clearly you never meant to show up that night, like you agreed. Unless you're going to tell me Rose locked you in a closet and went in your place?" Sarcasm seethes from me, and it's not an affect I adopt often.

"I'm involved with someone else. He didn't believe we weren't a real thing. I couldn't go that night. The photo call should've lasted an hour, so I begged Rose to go instead."

"Why the hell didn't you tell me the truth?"

"I was afraid you'd demand more appearances together." She hangs her head in shame. "Don't worry, I'll compensate you for non-performance. On the contract," she clarifies.

I don't fucking believe this. It's like an out-of-body experience, although I'm still alive and on planet earth.

"Damn, you're twisted. Do you really think you can fix the utter clusterfuck you've created by writing me a check? Get out my car. Please." I think I'm in shock.

She turns away from me, clicks the handle, and opens the door.

"I'm sorry, Wes," she tells me, standing by the car door in the driveway.

"Go to hell, Raelynn." I slide over and pull the door shut, then accelerate down her driveway, tires squealing.

CHAPTER THIRTY-THREE

ROSE

*T*GIF.

It's been a fantastic week.

With Raelynn due on set for Wes's video, my role officially ended, so I took a much needed few days off. After a spectacular Sunday with Wes, I hopped on a plane and flew to San Diego for a parents visit.

I needed to put some distance between me and Raelynn and muster support for my big decision to stop being her assistant and restart my music career.

The news thrilled my dad. A professor of media studies at a local university, he's always been on the technical side of creative fields. He felt I'd been wasting my talents and was delighted to see me put the college degree he's paid so much money for to good use.

My mother, well, she's another story.

Parents aren't supposed to have favorite children, but they do, even when they refuse to admit it. If I'm my father's favorite, Raelynn is Mom's. She owns her own PR firm, which specializes in crisis management. In her mind, my decision is a crisis.

For Raelynn, of course.

"I hope you're not flying by the seat of your pants. Have you got a job lined up?" she asked.

"Meeting a friend next week for lunch. Fingers crossed."

"And what about your sister? Have you told her?"

"Mom, she won't believe me until happens."

"Denise, they're both big girls now. Let them sort it out," my father told her.

When our final evening together rolled around, we made dinner together. Spicy shrimp tacos, a family favorite. The only thing missing was my twin sister. It made things bittersweet, since one of the reasons for my return was to get away from her.

By the end of my visit, it felt like we'd all been caught in a time warp. The mannerisms and conversations we had when I was back in high school all came flooding back, including one from my father that used to horrify me.

"So, you got any hot guys in your sights?" Dad asked after I passed him the creamy cilantro sauce.

Daaad! is how my fifteen-year-old self would've answered.

"Maybe. It's too new to say anything. Fingers crossed," is what twenty-six-year-old me told them.

Gasps of surprise replaced the healthy dose of banter

and stupid silliness that would've occurred in my teen years. It even prompted a hopeful glance exchanged between my parents.

"You do you, honey," my mother told me.

I guess things can change. Sometimes, they change for the better.

A loud metallic pop sounds as Wes's front door opens. I enter the house and reset the keyless entry system. He texted me the code during the flight back from San Diego and told me to come over.

I freaked out at first, but Wes insisted it's just easier to give out codes and then change them regularly.

I enter the dimly lit main level of the house. It's dark and desolate, and it makes me uncomfortable. Wes told me he'd be here by now. It doesn't feel right being in his house alone.

"Hello? Wes, are you here? It's Rose."

As I approach the stairs that lead to the lower level, unfamiliar chords from a too familiar guitar drift up from the closed basement door. I descend the stairs, and the door creaks as it opens. It's soundproof, because once I enter the lower level, the music is much louder than it was from the stairs only a few feet away.

It gets louder as I enter the room, and the unmistakable sound of Wes's voice breathes out new lyrics.

Like two sides of the same coin,
Tell me, which one is mine?

Win or lose, how does this end,
Who do I choose?

The lyrics unnerve me, and so does Wes's distant expression. When we've worked on music together, we often keep eye contact, even comment on things we like and don't like. Today, it's like I'm getting my own private concert. He's expressive and emotive as he tells me this story.

Despite the sense of dread that washes over me, leaving is impossible. I take my favorite seat on the sectional and face Wes. He sits on a stool in the center of the room, cradling his guitar. He knows I'm here but hasn't acknowledged it.

For Wes and many artists, music is a primary and often preferred form of communication. He runs through the chords one more time and stops abruptly.

"Like my new song?" he asks.

"I... don't know." I stammer. "How does it end?"

"Haven't figured that out yet." He pauses. "Want to help me?"

"Okay..." I fold my hands across my knees. "What's it's about?"

"I think you know."

My mouth goes dry, but I meet his gaze. "Why don't you tell me?"

"It's about a man who fell in love with a woman who turned out to be someone else."

"Is that a good or a bad thing?" I wonder aloud.

"It's a painful thing," he responds quietly.

Without warning, tears stream down my face. I hoped

this moment would never come. After he didn't recognize me twice, either from the time I sewed on his button or the day he brought flowers to Raelynn's house, I hoped he'd chalk up our night at HotZone to a one-time booty call with Raelynn that went nowhere.

"It doesn't need to be," I say.

Wes sets his guitar aside and reaches for a glass of amber liquid I hadn't noticed before. It's nearly empty, but he stares down at the last few drops and swirls them around the bottom of his glass.

"It was you that night at HotZone, not your sister." It's a statement, not a question.

"Yes." The admission comes easy.

"I thought she was finally coming to her senses." Wes huffs in disgust. "But something was off that night. I could feel it." He pauses a moment, then looks at me with strained blood-shot eyes. "Why'd you do it?"

"She couldn't go, or tell you why. She didn't want to do more appearances because she's seeing someone," I explain. "So, she sent me."

"Mmm." He knocks back the rest of his drink.

"How did you find out?" I ask.

"Your sister. I went to see her while you were at your parents. I felt like you were holding back with me because of her. I wanted to discuss our... past." He half laughs and grumbles.

"And she told you?"

"Oh, hell no. It was her the butterfly tattoo, absent on launch night. She tried to lie her way through it. Just like you."

"I haven't lied my way through this."

Wes throws his head back and howls with a wounded laugh.

It angers me.

HotZone wasn't my finest moment, but I felt I'd endured enough humiliation and atonement to live with it. I never realized until now that there's resentment on my part too.

"Go fuck yourself, Wes." The cold calm of my voice stops him short. "I didn't tell you because I kept hoping you'd remember me and realize what happened. You called me Angel Eyes that night at HotZone, like you did the night I sewed on your button."

"I don't remember that," he says in a hoarse voice.

"I do. Just like I remember you crying out my sister's name during sex. That was a particularly lethal dose of humiliation."

Wes groans and clutches the sides of his head.

"Of course, your speedy departure, bare-ass naked, carrying your clothes while you dressed on the run, stifled any confession I considered making." My voice cracks. "I remember thinking, 'if he treats an A-lister like Raelynn this way, how would he treat a normal girl like me?'"

"There were extenuating circumstances that night. Mind-blowing sex wasn't on the schedule. Raelynn would've known that."

"If you knew her as well you thought, you'd have known it too."

"Why did you sleep with me that night?" His tone is a mix of anger and bewilderment. "I thought you were someone else, but you knew who I was."

"Like I said, I hoped you remembered me."

"Suppose I had? The first time we met, you and I talked for five minutes." He glares at me. "The next time we're together you're swinging from the chandelier in a thong? What's that about?"

How do I tell him the truth?

That I'd been crushing on him for months through the texts I sent him from Raelynn's number? That I didn't expect to experience so much chemistry between us that night?

The only person I told was Nikki, in a desperate attempt to get my head on straight. She didn't press for details the way besties don't when they sense you need time to process things. I'm still processing.

I can't tell him and risk him trashing or trivializing what I felt that night. It was real for me. If wasn't for him, then I can't face it right now.

"I don't know. Maybe it was the costumes, the excitement. Or the way you reacted to everything I did that night."

"Maybe I'm a rock star and you were engaged in serious groupie behavior?" He glares at me, a mixture of disgust and disbelief.

"Groupie behavior? What about you?"

"Me?"

"How come you never figured out it was me at HotZone, even after the nights we spent together here? Are women all the same to you?" I lash out.

"No. Hell. No. You changed a lot between then and now."

"How?"

"For starters, your body." He glances off into nothingness. "It was much more… lush our first time."

"Lush? Is that code for fat?"

"Fuck." He glares at me, a mixture of disgust and disbelief. "I wish it were. Pliable. Fuckable. Irresistible. I won't forget it. Ever."

"And what about my sleepover?"

"The similarities unnerved me. But… you're an identical twin. You wore a costume that night. I didn't want to dwell on it. By the time you slept over, you were different. Everything was different." His voice is low and husky. "Your body, outlook, the music, the way we interacted. What we were… becoming to each other."

We sit in silence for a few moments. I rub my hands along the thighs of my jeans again. Wes shifts in his chair and sets his glass on the table. When our gazes meet, his eyes convey a sense of urgent expectation that matches my own.

So much need often follows so much truth.

"Which me did you like better?"

"Don't go there, Rose. It's not fair to either of us."

"You brought it up," I push. "How I was so different you couldn't believe I was the same person?"

"I liked you better when I knew who you were," he says with a bitter edge in his voice. "I tried like hell to make amends to your sister for behavior I deeply regretted. I wrestled with horrible feelings of guilt for being attracted to you. It made it impossible to not feel conflicted every time something good happened between us. How could you put us both through that?"

Tears run down and off the edge of my jawline.

"I tried so hard to make amends to both of you. I protected Raelynn's secret that night. I starved myself to work on your video when she wanted to quit, so you wouldn't be left high and dry. I shared the best of me with you, and you thought I was someone else."

"How can I trust you?" he asks.

"How do I forgive you?" I ask. "

"Maybe neither of us is with the person we thought we were with."

It breaks my heart to hear him say that. But I've always known it was possible things would turn out like this. What sucks is that I'd reached a point where I thought it unlikely.

How wrong I was.

"Maybe you're right."

CHAPTER THIRTY-FOUR

WES

"You like that one?" I ask.

The crowd roars in response.

"I've got a new one for you!"

More cheers.

There's a hundred and fifty, maybe two hundred people tops in here. It's a smallish crowd for us, but just what I need right now. We're at Seabreeze, the bar that my good friends Tony and Lola have owned for almost twenty years. They let us play here when we were nothing but wannabees.

After Rose and I called time on our relationship, the last conversation we had in bed has been messing with my head.

"Have you thought about my offer?" I asked, curled up in bed next to her. What better time to ask?

"Your offer?"

"To come work for the band after the video shoot is over."

Rosalie squirmed in my arms. "That's not a good idea, Wes."

"Why not?"

"For one, I'd be sleeping with the boss. And when things go sideways, it's the employee who ends up hitting the bricks."

"We're sleeping together now." I pulled her close as a reminder. "The video is nearly done and it's awesome. The music we've worked on is terrific. It doesn't make sense to not follow the path we're on and see where it leads."

"For you, maybe…"

It's occurred to me this past week, after I replayed this conversation several hundred times, that I was after more than Rosalie's musical talents. It was my way of asking her to stay without actually asking. Now whenever I try to play or sing, I'm inevitably drawn back to music and lyrics we worked on together.

Sucks, doesn't it?

That's why I'm here. Small intimate settings are my favorite venues to play. They don't pay the bills, but the atmosphere and repertoire you build with this kind of crowd is much different from the far more intense experience at a large venue.

Smaller venues are safer, more nurturing, and even

forgiving. I need that now. Because sometimes a particular song is not up to the scrutiny and intensity.

But you can't not play it.

"This one's a little new, a little rough. I started it with… someone else, and we uh, haven't been able to finish it."

I lean my electric guitar against the stool and adjust the microphone in front of me. Behind me, I hear Jai shuffle as he adjusts his bass. The song opens with me playing the guitar, but I've decided to sing it a cappella. That's not the way we practiced it, so the guys need to adjust on the fly in front of a live audience, which means they're probably a little pissed about now.

I'll apologize later.

It's nighttime now, but I'm still awake.
My covers are damp, my memories dank…

It's only the first verse, but I put all the power of my voice into it. I've got a broad natural range, but I belt my way up half an octave from the higher end with deliberate strain.

On the second verse, Jai begins to play in the original key we practiced instead of the one I'm belting. It's a clear sign that he's concerned. But when I don't continue with the second verse, Jai adapts to the new key.

I'm getting shit when this is over.

I know after hundreds of hours and tens of thousands of dollars in vocal coaching sessions that this is idiotic. If I strain too long, or if there's pain on my vocal cords, I risk serious damage to my voice.

I know, but it doesn't stop me. Because right now, I want it to hurt. I deserve it.

I don't want to feel that feeling again,
Of not being loved like I did back then.
The sleepless nights and unanswered texts
And lonely mornings filled with regret...

"Whoa! Yeah!" The audience cheers.

The lyrics remind me how hurt I am by what Rosalie's done. But I can't escape the fact that her behavior and my explanations for it make little sense.

She must have had self-serving motives. What other explanation can there be? Except her behavior has been anything but self-serving. If Rose was just a groupie, she'd have begged for another chance the night I confronted her. Instead, she'd stoically agreed that breaking up was the best thing.

If this was a calculated, cunning career move, why didn't she take the job I offered her? The credit and compensation alone would've been a boost to her career. Instead, she turned me down not once, but twice.

Truth be told, the only people who benefited from Rose's charade were me and her sister. Raelynn got out of our contract and control of her love life back. I got my video made and a bunch of songs salvaged that were headed for the dumpster.

When my throat starts to throb, I reached for my favorite Gibson guitar, no beat up acoustic on stage for me. I play what Rose and I composed together but create a new arrangement on the fly. My melody is a little slower and darker, and my ending is more ambivalent and less hopeful.

As I become engrossed in the music, I'm vaguely aware that Jai and Vince have stopped playing entirely. It's fitting that this song has become an improvised solo because it expresses feelings that are mine alone. Feelings I can't share but still want to be known.

Are you out there, Rose? Do you hear me?

CHAPTER THIRTY-FIVE

ROSE

"Thanks for the loan, Nikki. I'll pay you back as soon as I can." I haven't been paid for my work on the video yet, and Raelynn's payroll is going to be messed up this month.

"Don't worry about it right now. Fortunately, my roommate travels during the summer, and her share of the rent is paid up for the month." Nikki pauses. "Do you have any idea where you lost it?"

It's been a crazy week-and-a-half. Between parting ways with Wes and moving out of Raelynn's house for good, I've lost my phone.

"No. Between Wes and Raelynn's houses, the studio, and now here, I don't know where it's gone, and I'm not in a hurry to retrace my steps. When my new one arrives, I'll recover my contacts from the cloud. In the meantime, being free from the dread of taking unwanted calls is a welcome relief."

The downside is that I'll never know if Wes tried to call me or not.

"I don't blame you," Nikki hesitates. "Do you want to tell me what happened yet? Or do you need more time?"

The last thing I want to do is discuss it, but I do owe Nikki an explanation. This week morphed into the single worst of my life. Ever. Hands down. Through it all, Nikki's proven to be the loyal friend we all hope will go the distance for us, even as we pray to never need to lean so hard on someone.

But I did. I went there.

In the space of five days, I completed one job, quit another, alienated my sister, and ended my cushy living arrangement in one of the most expensive cities on the planet. I also broke up with a man I'd grown to love.

Screw my life.

Raelynn left town for a work gig the day before I broke up with Wes. For the next forty-eight hours, I was alone. I stayed in bed and alternated between staring at the ceiling and counting the carpet loops.

When she returned, sympathetic understanding was not part of her agenda. Angry, accusatory, and self-absorbed best described her demeanor from the moment her designer luggage hit the tile floor of the foyer.

"Rosalie? Rosalie!" she yelled from the bottom of the stairs.

I didn't answer right away. What was the point? She'd eventually come up here and find me. I can still hear the furious *tap, tap, tap* of her heels as she marched up the polished stone staircase and down the hall to my bedroom.

"What the hell were you thinking?" she shrieked after throwing my bedroom door open.

Somehow, I sat up in bed, but I took my time with it. "Not now. Please," I told her.

"You slept with Wes Anders and let him think you were me?" She was furious.

So was I. Something inside me snapped.

Raelynn's 'me good, you bad' spin on things wasn't acceptable. Not this time, or ever again.

"I have, no, I want, a life that is different from yours. One that I can live with." I stood up and faced her, unshowered, wearing three-day-old clothes. "As for Wes Anders, I'm done apologizing for what happened that night, especially to you. You asked me to go there in your place that night. You are far from blameless."

"I never asked you to sleep with him."

"No." I glared at her. "You asked me to keep your secret, and I did. You should've worn that idiotic costume and attended like you promised, then dealt with the blow-back from Sergio like a grown-up instead of relying on teenage tactics. Instead of you putting your problems on me, like you've always done."

"That's not fair," she yelled.

"It sure as hell isn't" I agreed. "I've got bigger problems to worry about than you being sued for the terrible way you treated Wes. And me."

"This wouldn't be such a disaster if you'd been more careful and controlled yourself." She shakes her head. "You were working."

"When do I not work for you? You charge into my room on a weekend morning, telling me who I can sleep with, while you complain that I didn't put your interest ahead of mine that night at HotZone. Not only is that BS, but you had no right to expect that from me."

I leapt off the bed and headed to the closet. I pulled the accordion doors open with vigor and unburied my large, beat up suitcase. A purple hard shell with duct tape decal band-aids covering the corner cracks.

Battered and bruised, it'd been a graduation present from my parents, and it kept its authentic character despite years of use and abuse. My authentic character. Colorful, cracked, creative, and ready to travel, so unlike the designer luggage Raelynn uses.

I wouldn't have it any other way.

"What are you doing?" she asked.

"I've stayed in this job out of guilt for failing at my career and living here when I needed help. But mostly because I was waiting for you to be my sister again. Someone who was kind, supportive, and gave a damn about my happiness. Just like I did for you. But the longer I wait, the clearer it is that won't happen. You've always put yourself first. Now I'm going to live by your example.

I quit."

Since then, Nikki's been more supportive than Rae ever has been. I couldn't have done this without her help.

"Wow. You really quit and moved out. Your entire life up in flames."

"Long overdue. Raelynn and I reached a point where we both felt the other was over demanding and under appreciative. It wasn't healthy for either of us. Someday we'll patch things up, but right now I need to get my own life in order."

Nikki gives me a nod of approval. "Sometimes in life you need to press the eject button and start over. It's hard and scary, but it's the only choice when you can't stay where you are and you don't like where you're going."

"True that. Thanks again."

"What are your plans?" she asks.

"Find a job yesterday. I'm meeting Brad for lunch in a few days. Remember him? We worked together at my first job. I hope he's got good news. If he doesn't, I'll need to start a cold search. How long can I stay here?"

"My roommate received a grant for history teachers that covers her through the summer. She's in Europe visiting medieval castles, and she won't be back until before school starts."

"About six weeks then?" I ask.

"Five. After that we can squeeze out a week or two on the sofa bed."

"Let's hope it doesn't come to that."

"Let's," Nikki agrees. "What about Wes?"

"I've lost his trust," I answer. "It's over."

"Are you sure there's nothing you can do?"

"No." I refuse to let myself hope. It's a self-imposed form of torture. "He doesn't understand what I did, or why. I regret not telling the truth, and it's easy to blame everything on me. But I'm not the only one at fault, and I certainly gained nothing except a broken heart."

"Did you ever tell him about the texts?"

"No." I shake my head. "No."

"Maybe you should."

"Why? Will another confession make it better? I don't think so. And I'm done with the self-flagellation. Sometimes deception backfires."

"Are you going to be okay?"

"I hope so."

CHAPTER THIRTY-SIX

WES

My feet chuff against the stone steps that lead up to Raelynn's front porch. I ring the doorbell and moments later my head jerks back in surprise when she answers it herself.

There's bed head. Lots of bed head.

Judging from that, plus the cutoff denim shorts, halter top, and no makeup, she's planned a quiet day at home.

"Wow, answering your own door. What's next?" I ask

Raelynn glares at me. "Good help is a little hard to find right now." She folds her arms "What do you want, Wes?"

"Rose left her phone at my place." I pull the ceramic white phone from my back pocket "I'm here to return it."

Raelynn unfolds her arms and sighs. "I guess we've

got some loose ends to tie up. Will you come in for a while?" she asks.

While I'm eager to put this entire ordeal behind me and get on with my life, having this conversation on the front porch doesn't appeal to me either. I pull off my sunglasses and follow her inside.

As we pass the marble table where Rose and I arranged flowers together, I mentally kick myself. The intense chemistry between us the first time I met the real Rose confused and tortured me.

Knowing it was she who spent that spectacular night with me at the launch party only makes me angrier at myself. How did I not realize the truth right away? Maybe I was so determined to hold onto my fantasies that I ignored the reality up in my face.

Her. Me. Us. Fuck.

Raelynn leads me into a large custom kitchen and gestures toward the massive island in the center. On the side nearest to me, there's an odd pile of personal items. A jewelry box, a songwriter's notebook, and a small makeup bag.

"What's all this?" I ask?

"Those are Rose's things. Nikki's coming by to pick them up." Raylan's expression is gaunt and tight-lipped. "She doesn't live here anymore."

Damn.

The news hits me like a punch to the stomach. I didn't realize how eager I was to see her until now.

"Where did she go?" I ask?

"She won't say." She swallows hard. "We had a major blowout after I confronted her. Rose took what could fit in the car and left. After a dozen calls, and God knows how many texts, she messaged me from Nikki's phone and said she was fine, with a new job and a place to stay."

"She found a job? Doing what? Where?"

"I don't know where she works or lives," Raelynn answers. Visibly shaken, she folds her hands on top of the counter and stares unfocused at the tile floor. It's clear the state of their relationship upsets her. How could two people so close hurt each other like this?

That's when it hits me. I know the answer to my own question.

It's a fear of losing what we have and being worried we're settling at the same time. The most fucked up part is when you realize that even if the person you love doesn't return your feelings, you'd take them anyway. Because being with them is all that matters.

I feel that way about Rose, but how does she feel about me?

Reluctantly, I take a seat on one of the island stools with deliberate slowness. I place Rose's cell phone next to her notebook on the counter, then fold my hands together.

"We've always been so close," she murmurs, still focused on nothing. "At least, I always thought so. God, I really screwed up this time, and I didn't even know it."

My hands raise in a pleading gesture. "Raelynn, you shouldn't confide in me about your problems with Rose. I'm not objective. And sorry, not sorry."

"I owe you an apology." Raelynn takes a deep breath. "It was me who insisted that Rose attend your launch party in my place. She wasn't happy about it. Not at all."

"She mentioned that," I reply. The whys and hows don't concern me right now. I just want to see Rose again.

"There's someone in my life, and I want him to stay," Raelynn confesses.

"I can relate to that."

"Sergio D'Souza." She says his name out loud, as if it explains everything.

The name recognition takes a moment.

"The CEO of LLG?" I ask.

D'Souza's Lakshmi Luxury Group, LLG amassed a fortune buying up obscure brands in Europe and the US, then marketing them as luxury high-end brands in emerging Asian markets.

"Yeah," she answers. "Sergio didn't believe our relationships was fake. And the way you flirted with me made things worse."

My chin drops to my chest. "Seriously? The flirting would have never happened without all those texts you sent me. Get over yourself."

"Texts?" She sounds confused. "Talk about using any excuse. My rare texts were nothing but polite and professional."

I blow out a frustrated breath and stand. Raelynn Tailor is delusional, and my trip to Fantasyland is over. "Now everything's my fault? Whatever. This conversation is over, have a nice life. All of you."

"Wes, wait. Please." Raelynn comes around to my side of the kitchen island. "I know I'm not blameless. I won't try to convince you otherwise. What I hoped to get from you is the phone number of your music video editor. I need copies of the final footage before it's released. I'm sorry to bother you. Rose usually handles these things for me, and well, you know…" She gives me a half-apologetic shrug.

We agreed to this, and since I want to get the hell out of here, I whip out my phone, find the editor's name in my contacts and send her a text.

That's when something fucked up occurs.

Rose's ceramic white phone lights up with a text notification. I lurch across the end of the kitchen island to grab the phone. Before it goes dark again. I glimpse my text on her screen.

"Thanks, I need to text my agent." Raelynn retreats into her own world, fingers tapping the screen with quick, repeated motions.

"What just happened?" A chill runs down my spine.

Raelynn looks at Rose's phone with a dismissive nod. "It went to both of my lines."

"Both of your lines?"

"Yes, don't you have an assistant who takes calls for you?"

"Yes…" I reply. "But he has his own number, and if I don't answer calls, they forward to his phone."

"That's too much work for me. I don't want to screen calls and decide which ones to answer, that's Rose's," she takes a deep breath, "my assistant's job. I have multiple phone numbers and a system of what number we give to whom and who answers each one."

My gaze darts from Raelynn to Rose's phone and back to mine. I dial Raelynn's number from my contacts list and Rose's phone lights up again.

"Is that your number?" I hold up my phone for Raelynn to inspect.

"Mmm, hmm," she answers and returns to her text.

I search up my contacts again and dial the number I have stored for Rose. The white ceramic phone vibrates on the counter.

"Is that your number?"

Raelynn looks up from her text messages again, annoyed. "They're all my numbers."

Alarm bells ring inside my head, but I'm not sure why, at least not yet.

"What about text messages?"

"What about them?"

"Can you see the text messages sent from every one of your numbers?"

"Only if they're sent through the app you download from the phone company, which neither of us do. We use the apps that come with our phones."

I steady myself against the countertop. Looking back, I realize that I've never tried to call Rosalie. We've spoken on the phone, but only when I tried to reach Raelynn. When Rose answered, I just assumed the call was forwarded like it is between me and Felix.

My hand shakes as I open the text app on my phone and go to what I believed was Raelynn's private phone number. Shared jokes, words of encouragement, good and bad days, favorite music, quiet nights at home, not quite alone.

"Raelynn, you said this was your number." I point to the top of my screen, and she looks up once again. "Did you send me these texts?"

Raelynn glances up at my phone. Her brows crease before her eyes widen in shock.

"Oh my God." She covers her mouth with her hand, then reaches for my phone. I let her pull it from my grasp. "Wes, I swear to you I never sent these."

I steady myself against the countertop.

Raelynn rakes her long hair several times, then returns my phone. "It all makes sense now. The too-personal comments. Your persistence and confusion at my disinterest. I thought it was just rock star ego. But all that time, you thought I sent you these."

I give her a distant nod, then reach across the kitchen island and grab Rosalie's phone.

"I need to find Rose."

"I can't wait that long. Give it to me." Raelynn's hand waves back toward her.

"Do you know her passcode?"

"Even better." Raelynn gives me a thumbs up. "Identical twins, remember?"

"Fingerprints?" I ask

"No, they're too different, even for us. I've tried." Raelynn sounds disappointed. "Facial recognition. That's a whole other thing."

"Are you sure it's not an invasion of privacy?" I want to see Rose's texts but not without her knowledge.

"Not for me it isn't. That's my employer-provided phone and those are my numbers. Hand it over."

Reluctantly, I drop it on the counter and Raelynn swoops it up. She holds it up in the air, presses the button, and poses for the camera. Seconds later, the home screen unlocks. A list of phone numbers appears, and Raelynn selects the second one on the list. The in-house text app lives at the bottom of the next page, and she opens it and scrolls through the contacts.

"Is that your number?" Raelynn holds Rose's phone up to me and I check the number listed in my contact details.

"That's me," I admit.

When she touches my name in the app, months of texts appear. From over her shoulder, I glance at a few exchanges before backing away toward the counter. I know what they say because I wrote them.

"What are you doing?" I ask. "I told you, they're mine."

"Going back to the beginning. And checking some other things."

"I can see why you and your sister have issues. You're too much in each other's business."

She ignores me, preoccupied as she scrolls through the texts until the phone stops showing new ones. She reads intently for a few moments, then scrolls with disinterest. This goes on for about ten minutes until she sets Rosalie's phone back on the counter.

"It looks like it started out innocently enough. She answered some mundane questions. At one point, you commented about another singer and things went from there. This shouldn't have happened, but I understand how it did."

I nod in resignation.

"The texts ended the night of your launch party. That's when you slept together?"

I nod again.

"For what it's worth, she's got several A-Listers in her contacts whom she deals with on my behalf. Some of them… I didn't pay her enough. This is not a regular thing for her, I checked. I believe she liked you and felt like confiding in either of us was impossible. As her sister, I'm ashamed of that. I'm sorry to both you."

My mind flows in a dozen different directions. The texts. The night at HotZone. Her work on the video. Her musical talents. Those nights in my bed. That was all a SINGLE woman rather than two exceptional ones.

This… deception wasn't her finest moment. Rose tried to help Raelynn with her love life problems. But us? All I know for sure is she didn't deceive me for personal gain. I liked her, and it was mutual. The rest is just the rest.

Why didn't she tell me?

"Raelynn, I need to find your sister."

CHAPTER THIRTY-SEVEN

ROSE

"*How's* it going, Rose?" Brad asks as he enters the studio. I can't hear him because of my headphones, but I've become an excellent lipreader.

I smile and raise a single finger in the air, then save my work and remove the bulky studio headset.

"So far, so good. I'm working on a split for the second episode of the show."

My split involves separating the human voice from the instrumental music of a song so that the actors in the show and singer in the background music aren't speaking at the same time.

"Can you handle the DAW software?"

"I'm getting better. It's not the one I normally use, but

I did work with it in school. Is this one considered more professional?"

"Well, more old school, anyway. And Carl's pretty old school."

"Not to mention incredibly talented. I've learned more working here for two weeks than in an entire college semester. Thank you for coming through on this for me, Brad. It means more than you know."

He shrugs and a shock of salt and pepper curly hair falls across his clear plastic glasses. "You were always talented, dedicated, and picked things up fast. It makes my job much easier."

Brad is our senior assistant composer and recording manager. In his mid-thirties, he's about seven years older than me. He's worked in the field since before I met him at my last job. He's moved steadily up the career ladder, while I'm grateful to have an entry-level job again.

My new job as an assistant composer is at the same level I started at four years ago. But at least it's paid work in my field, which is tremendous. We're working on a limited series of a television show for a major studio's streaming channel. It runs for twelve episodes, which means I'll be looking for work again soon, but hopefully not too soon.

"Thank you. I'll try not to disappoint anyone," I promise. "Did you need something, or were you just checking to make sure the studio hadn't burned down?"

"Yes," Brad snaps his fingers. "Carl wants to see you before lunch. He'll be down in a few minutes, so don't leave before you see him."

"Is something wrong?"

"I don't think so," Brad says with a smile. "I'd stick around, but I'm meeting my wife for lunch." He turns to leave, then stops at the door. "You're lucky to be working for someone like Carl Christensen. Learn how he works, copy it, and make it yours. Make it better if you can. That's where the real value of being an assistant lies," he says.

"Thanks. Have a nice lunch," I call out as he leaves.

Oh my God.

Our boss is an independent, award-winning composer hired to write music for a major studios' streaming channel. He's the type of man who says good morning in the hall, but if he's got a technical or schedule question there are way more senior people to ask.

What does Carl want to discuss with me?

I straighten up my desk and throw a paper coffee cup away. I reach for my phone, then toss it in a desk draw right before Carl enters the studio. A man in his mid-fifties, he's dressed in typical workday attire. A pressed dress shirt, with the collar of a white tee peeking out from under the top button, dark pants, and these half-tennis, half-orthopedic shoes that he wears every day.

He strolls in at a casual pace, his hands clasped behind his back as he walks. It's typical for him, but it always makes me wonder if he's got something hidden.

Carl stops at the two other workstations and appears to inspect them, but his hands never move from behind his back. I haven't worked here long enough to read him, but his silence and non-acknowledgement of me add to my feelings of awkwardness.

"Good morning, Mr. Christensen. Is there something I can help you with?" I try to sound calm.

"Call me Carl." He looks up from one of the workstations. "I just stopped by for a chat. Is now a good time?"

"Of course."

He nods and takes a seat at the side of my desk, where the large computer monitors don't block our view of each other. Then he stretches out his long, lanky legs and folds his hands in his lap.

"I went out to the Seabreeze recently. It's bar that hosts live musical performances. Have you been there?" he asks.

"I don't think so."

"Not my usual scene, but I was meeting a friend."

There's an awkward pause. I have no idea where he's going with this.

"Um, did you have a nice time?" I ask.

"Yes, but that's not my point." He studies me carefully.

"You've lost me Mr., uh, Carl."

"Jester's Edge gave an unannounced performance while I was there."

"Oh wow, how... unexpected. That must've been nice." I give a nervous chuckle. I don't understand why he's asking me about Jester's Edge, but it has my stomach twisted into knots.

"Wes Anders performed a new song and credited an unnamed songwriter in his monologue. The name of the song was 'All I Never Wanted.'"

What?

I struggle to keep my eyes from bulging and my

mouth from dropping wide open. I fold my hands on the desk and nod.

"A few days later, he released it as a single. Rosalie M. Tailor was given a songwriters' credit."

"I was?" I blurt out.

"Then it is you," Carl confirms. "Why the hell didn't you mention this in your job interview?"

Oh. *That.*

Because I'm in love with Wes Anders and he doesn't want me. As hard as I work and try to accept what will never be, I still cry about it at night. Every. Single. Night.

"I had no idea he was going to perform or release the song." I lean back in my chair.

"How did you end up writing music with Jester's Edge?" Carl asks.

Keep this professional, I warn myself. "I worked on their last music video."

Carl's eyes widen. "You have music video experience? Production? Post-production? I don't understand why none of this is on your resume."

"They hired me as a body double for the video. I didn't do any sound work."

"Except write a song?"

"Well, I did more than that. Some musical arrange-ments," I add when Carl's eyebrows shoot up. "There was no formal agreement, more like relaxing after long days on set. I'm sorry if you feel blindsided, but the fact is, it was a short-term thing, and now it's over."

"What's over?"

"That chapter of my life. Listen, I don't have insider connections to the band or their label. I can't arrange any

introductions or hook you up with sweet deals on synchro-
nization contracts, and I refuse to set those expectations
and then disappoint everyone. I'm a composer, and I need
to know if I'm good enough all on my own, because I
suck at self-promotion."

Carl throws his head back and laughs. "You sure do.
In a city where people over promote and under deliver, it's
a bizarre and refreshing change."

Hearing myself out loud, I know I'm talking about
more than just writing songs, but every word is the truth.
*Please don't let the truth cost me my job. It's already cost
me too much.*

"Is that a… compliment?" I ask when he stops
laughing.

"From me? Yes. Although I'll deny it if anyone asks."
Carl leans across the desk. "I hired you for two reasons.
One, Brad thinks you're talented. He runs my recording
sessions, and what he wants, he gets. But it was your
experience as a PA for a demanding, in-demand, A-list
celebrity with expectations as brutal as her schedule that
caught my attention. Apparently, you've got talents far
beyond connections with the best coffee shops and
smoothing the most ruffled of feathers."

"Damn right I do."

"Good to know." Carl stands. "I believe in fair pay, so
expect a raise at your next payday."

"A raise? For what?"

"It's clear you'll be doing far more than making coffee
and running errands. Besides, I hope to stave off any
poachers."

"Poachers?"

"People who'd offer you jobs, some for your talent, some for the reasons you've tried to avoid. Word gets around, just like it did. Have a look at your next paycheck before you make any decisions. I hope you'll stick around."

"Thank you, Carl." My voice is hoarse and heavy with emotion.

"Welcome aboard, Rosalie."

CHAPTER THIRTY-EIGHT

ROSE

"*M*y treat tonight, Nikki." I wave the server to our regular table.

"Are we celebrating something?" she asks.

"Yes we are. My new job, and my raise. I feel like I'm on the right path for the first time in years."

It's an innocuous after work Wednesday at *Lola's Place*. Nikki wanted to meet somewhere for a drink, and I needed to share some news with her. *Lola's Place* was the natural choice. It's busy here without being overcrowded and hectic, but that will change in the next hour. I want to enjoy the atmosphere while it lasts.

"Congratulations!" Nikki says. "But why? I mean, you just started working there."

Our usual server takes Nikki's order for a californication and a mojito for me. It gives me time to think about Nikki's question, which I need because I'm stilled stunned.

"As strange as it sounds, I think it was for just being myself," I reply.

"That's bizarre," she says, then gives me an apologetic look. "You know what I mean."

"You've got that right." I blow out a breath. "Wes Anders released a single and gave me a songwriters' credit. My boss found out about it." I swirl my drink. "He appreciated me not name dropping or embellishing my qualifications."

"Wes did that?"

"That's what my boss told me."

Our drinks arrive and I indulge in a long slow sip, then let it work its magic.

"Have you listened to it?" she asks.

"No. About a week ago I was in the shower when the 'music inspired by my playlist' played Jester's Edge's Cyclone." I shake my head, unnerved at the recollection.

"Cyclone? Is that the one he starts out with a sexy scream?"

"Yeah. It upset me so much I jumped out of the shower fully lathered and ran to my bedroom and shut it off. I've avoided the radio and random streaming ever since."

Nikki stares at me for a few minutes in disbelief before taking a long sip of her drink. Then she takes out her phone, lays it on the table between us, and taps open her music app.

"What are you doing?" I slide the phone back over to her.

"Maybe Wes is trying to tell you something. Maybe you should listen."

I throw my head back against the wooden top of the booth. It makes a painful thud sound, but I barely notice. "What else is there to say? I deceived him, he doesn't trust me anymore. Believe me, it's on auto-replay in my head."

Nikki twists her body, props a bent arm on the wooden table, and rests her chin on it. "Does he know your new number?"

"No."

"Have you called him?"

I laugh in disbelief. "No."

"Text?"

My head bangs against the booth a second time. "Not in a million years."

"Then you're not leaving too many options."

"Maybe I'm not strong enough yet," I snap. "Maybe I've been so wrapped up in how bad I made him feel that it's taken me a while to realize that he hurt me too and that I need time to deal with it, on my own terms and timetable."

"Oh, shit." Nikki hunches down in the booth and ducks her head.

"What is it? Nikki?" I demand.

"My timing sucks. I didn't know about Wes and the songwriting thing and your struggle to process it all." Nikki gives my hand a gentle pat. "I wanted to meet tonight and tell you I saw Raelynn. She wants to talk."

Raelynn.

It's been almost three weeks since I quit working for her and moved out. In some ways it's felt like a long vacation. One I'm not ready to end. I've been free to make choices without having to put her first. I've done what's best for me for the first time in years.

My life feels like it belongs to me again.

Although I love my sister, I'm still learning how to set limits in our relationship. It's hard because for so long she steamrolled over my emotions and ambitions. Am I strong enough to prevent that from happening again?

"I'm not sure that's a good idea."

"She'll be here in five minutes."

"What? Since when are you Team Raelynn?"

"Come on, Rose. Really?"

I fold my arms and glare at Nikki. It never seems right to be mad at her, so I quickly redirect my focus to the coaster on the table while she speaks.

"When I went to pick up your stuff, of course Raelynn realized I knew where you lived and worked. She asked about you and wanted your new number. I wasn't comfortable sharing that with her."

"Thanks."

"I told her we were meeting here tonight."

Speechless, my jaw drops in horror.

"It was the only way for me to respect your privacy and do what I thought was right."

"And what do you think is right?"

Nikki rubs her temples. "You need to talk to your sister. I've known you both a long time, and this rift has been hard on her too."

"You think I should see her because she's having a hard time?" My voice rises in distress.

"No. I think there are people close to you who are ready to admit they've made mistakes too. That blaming you for everything has gotten them nothing and nowhere." Nikki nods. "If your sister's ready to apologize, you need to hear it."

"Is that why she wants to meet? To say she's sorry?"

"Lord, I hope so. But there's no such thing as a guarantee. We're talking about Raelynn, right?" she laughs in disgust. "But hey, you can always leave here anytime you want."

Beneath the table, I feel my heel tap against the floor, a physical response to my uncertainty. An evening with Raelyn is not what I'd envisioned, but I'm ready to handle a tough conversation in a crowded bar.

"Okay, Nikki. I'll do it."

Nikki takes a deep breath, then sends a text.

"May I sit down?" Raelynn asks.

Even in jeans and a shirt, she still looks like a model. As she stands at the head of the table, she draws several curious glances.

"Go ahead," I nod, folding my hands on the tabletop.

She slides in across from me, just as Nikki stands up.

"The server looks a little busy now. I'll head up to the bar for a refill. Anyone need something?" she asks.

"I'm good," I answer.

"I'll wait for the server to come back around. Thanks for asking though." Raelynn replies.

As we sit in silence, I vow not to be the one who speaks first.

"You look good, Rose," Raelynn finally says. "Happy?"

"Not yet," I admit. "But I'm working on it. How about you?"

"Working on it," she admits. "Feels like a long way to go some days."

"I know that feeling." We smile at each other.

Raelynn removes her dark glasses and sets them on the table. Whatever she came to say is hard for her. I'm not sure I want to hear it, but she's my sister, my twin, and her anxiety affects me too.

"Just say what you want to, already," I tell her. "It can't get much worse."

"I need to say I'm sorry, and it's really hard for me." She nods to herself, like she's working up courage. "There were so many things about you that I took for granted. Because we were close, I didn't always respect your privacy, or your choices. And because you worked for me, I did take your support for granted. That was wrong."

"I'm sorry I quit so suddenly," I reply. "I can always find another boss, but never another sister. And you didn't feel like my sister anymore, because I couldn't tell you stuff I wanted to tell you without upsetting my boss. It became untenable."

"You were right to quit, and brave, too." Raelynn's eyes well with tears, but she keeps them in check. "I want my sister back. And I want the chance to be as good a sister to you as you were to me."

"That's all I ever wanted from you, Rae. You helped me when I lost my job. I've never denied that. But I tried hard to make it up to you, too."

'You did. Thank you." Now her tears are rolling, and it hurts me to see her like that."

"It means a lot to hear you say that, Raelynn."

"It means a lot that you'll listen to me say it," she replies.

"Please don't cry. Seeing you cry makes me cry too."

"I can't help it right now." Raelynn stands, slides out of the booth, and comes to sit beside me.

She wraps her arms around me and gives me a kiss on the cheek, the way she did when we were children. It makes me cry. She holds me tight for a moment, then I hug her, too.

"You know, Rose, you're not the only person I owe an apology to."

"I have no doubt." I'm half serious, half joking.

Raelynn swallows. "Wes. I need to tell you about him."

"What about him? Did something happen?"

"Happen? No, nothing happened," she assures me. "The band is having a wrap party for *Pretty Little Liar.* They want to invite you, but they don't know where you live or how to get in touch. So, they asked me to extend an invitation."

"Oh, Wow." I fold my elbows on the table. "I don't know if I can do that. Are you going?"

"Yes."

When she sees my surprise, she raises her hand and explains.

"Wes didn't invite me. He called Sergio and invited him. Then he asked Sergio if he could bring me. Sergio is eager for us to attend. Yes, we're going."

"Whew. I guess so." I laugh nervously. "I hope no one's expecting me to be a plus one?'

"No. It's cocktail attire. I'll text Nikki and give her the details, until you're ready to share your phone number with me."

"I can give you my number now," I tell her.

"Please don't. Not yet. The urge to text you a million times a day is still there. Until I'm in a better place, let's keeps things the way they are," Raelynn insists.

"Okay then." It sounds weird, but I'm happy at the prospect of Raelynn's self-imposed boundaries.

"Thanks," she says. "You know where to find me if you need something."

"I do."

She nods. "You'll let me know about the party?"

"As soon as I decide."

CHAPTER THIRTY-NINE

WES

"*J*hope you know what you're doing." Vince claps me on the shoulder with his bear-like hand.

"Me too," I answer, trying to hide the fact that I'm nervous as hell.

"Well, if things don't work out the way you want, at least it was a helluva party."

"Yeah. Right."

The wrap party for Pretty Little Liar is a bit unusual. We've chosen a local, trendy, posh boutique hotel as the venue, while trying to keep the guest list small and intimate. It's cast, crew, and plus ones, which should keep attendance at less than a hundred. It's a private party, no media or retained photographer.

All pretty elaborate, considering the whole fucking reason I arranged this was for a chance to see Rose again.

There's hotel staff stationed outside the doors of our rented venue who are tasked with checking names off the guest list. But instead of mingling with the guests, I've stationed myself out here, hoping to see Rose the instant she arrives.

Damn it, where is she?

Raelynn confirmed via text that she'd extended my invitation with no hint of Rose's response. She's not here either, so I can't ask her.

"Have you seen Rose yet?" Vince asks.

"No."

"Is she coming?"

"I hope so."

"You don't know?" Vince asks.

"No," I admit. "Neither Raelynn nor I have her new phone number."

Vince blows out a breath. "You went through all this without extending a personal invitation and or knowing if she'll even show?" Vince makes a *tut-tut-tut* sound that makes me want to smack him. "Whipped, whipped like a dog. How the mighty have fallen."

"Are you here to gloat?" I ask.

"Hell, no. I'm here for moral support."

"Moral support?" I choke. "That's not really your thing, is it, Vince?"

"You got me." He raises his hands in surrender. "I'm a selfish SOB. But I've also been in this business longer than you, and, hell, we both know you're the real reason I'm still in it." His voice grows low and serious. "Thanks to you, I not only get a paycheck, but it's a fucking huge one. So, when I see you doing things like this," he waves at the private screening room next to the dining area with the open bar and elaborate buffet, "to have a conversation with a woman you're not sure will show up, consider me your self-appointed, self-serving wingman."

"Where's Jai? Can he be my wingman?"

"Sorry, he's too busy chasing Nikki's sweet ass every-where and trying not to be obvious about it."

"Nikki? Rose's friend? Since when?"

"You really are out to lunch. Since day one. She doesn't give him much play, though. It's kind of fun to watch."

"Nikki's here? Where? Has she seen Rose?" I ask.

"No, but I have." Vince nods in the direction of the hotel lobby. "There's your girl."

I draw an audible breath when Rose comes into view. She's in a sleeveless turquoise sheath dress that hugs her body. Dark brown hair falls in loose waves that frame her angular, freckled face. She's arrived alone, and the look on her face suggests bailing is a serious possibility.

"Go on," Vince says. "Put us all out of your misery. Hurry."

"See ya."

I'm about twenty yards away when she notices me. When I come to a stop in front of her, Rose's expression transforms from uncertain to a strange mix of regret and desire. That X-rated mouth parts, and her tongue slides over those perfect, white front teeth. The only thing that stops me from owning that mouth is the sad, regretful expression in her eyes.

"Hello, Wes."

"Rose. Thank you so much for coming." I want to pull her close and say so many things to her. Instead, my hands open, palms up in front, and I extend them to her.

Rose stares down at them before she places a single palm on top of my mine, like she's trying to shake my hand, only she remains motionless. Awkward as hell, but impossible to be anything else at the moment.

I cradle her hands between both of mine. "I didn't know if you'd come."

"Me either. I thought you never wanted to see me again."

"I was upset that night. I regret what I said."

"I don't blame you. I lied," she admits.

"I wish it never happened. But I'm human enough to know there are far more selfish, sinister reasons to lie than trying to protect someone or avoid hurt and humiliation."

Rose's hand wriggles in mine, and her eyes dart around the room. She's ready to bolt, so I change the subject.

"You look great. Beautiful." It's not false flattery. Her skin glows and she's gained some weight back. "Rae says you're doing well. A new job and a place to live?"

"Yes. I've got a nice place and great job."

"That's fantastic. Do you mind if I ask what you do?"

"I am an assistant composer for Carl Christianson. We're working on a television limited series for a studio streaming service."

The news is bittersweet for me. While I'm pleased to hear of her success, it stings because it feels like she's moved on a little too easily, and maybe she hasn't left in any room in her life for us. After what happened, is it fair to blame her?

"It's an excellent opportunity. You're immensely talented and I know you'll thrive there."

"Speaking of thriving... thank you for the credit on 'All I never wanted'."

The songwriters' credit was fair, and I have no regrets about sharing it. But I'll admit the rushed release of the single track was an attempt to make amends, and I hoped when she learned about it, she'd contact me. Much, much sooner than now.

Does she not understand that? Or does she just not give a damn?

"It's like I promised. You'll always get fair credit for work you do with us." I hesitate, then plunge in headfirst. "But I'm surprised you didn't reach out earlier. The song's doing pretty well."

"I haven't heard it." Rose's body stiffens.

"What?" I must've misunderstood her.

"Other people told me about it," she says. "But I'm not ready."

"Not ready? I don't understand," I reply.

"I'm not ready to be all 'you never wanted.' And you're not the only musician who processes emotions and events through their work." She gives me a direct stare. "I'm not ready."

She's right. I performed and released the song as a way to process my own emotions. But it's her song as much as mine, and she wrote it for her own reasons. All things considered, it was insensitive to release it without giving her a heads up.

I'm about to say as much when we're interrupted.

"Rose? Rose," Raelynn calls to her as she enters the lobby.

She's not alone.

Literally attached at the hip is the manicured hand of Sergio D'Souza. They make a stunning couple, Raelynn in her designer cocktail dress and open toe-pumps, and Sergio in a pewter suit with paisley tie. When Raelynn speeds up to reach her sister, de Souza's hand doesn't leave her body.

"Hello Raelynn," Rose replies.

"I thought you were going to call me. Did you come alone? How did you get here?"

"Just me and my Uber driver."

"You should've ridden with us. Sergio's driver could've picked you up."

"I like to come and go without explanations or permission. Uber is fine for me, thanks," Rose tells her.

Raelynn starts to speak, but Sergio cuts her off. "I think your sister's taken enough flack, Raelynn." Sergio clears throat. "Rose, if you want a ride, just let us know. It's no trouble either way."

"You must be Sergio. I'm Rose." She extends a hand.

Sergio removes his hand from Raelynn's hip and moves forward to take Rose's. "It's nice to finally meet you, Rose. I regret not insisting on an introduction sooner. My apologies."

Raelynn clears her throat and changes the topic to me.

"You two haven't met either. Sergio, this is Wes. Wes, Sergio."

"Anders." Sergio extends his hand and greets me.

"You need to call me Wes, because I sure as hell aren't calling you D'Souza." I give his hand a firm shake.

He shrugs in response. "Sergio."

"Glad you could accept my invitation."

"I wouldn't miss it," he assures me.

"The video screening should start in about fifteen minutes," I announce while checking my watch. "Perhaps you and Raelynn would enjoy a drink before it starts? The open bar is through the second set of doors."

"I could use a drink," Raelynn says.

"Sounds like a good idea. We'll see you in there." Sergio nods at us and leads Raelynn to the bar.

"Rose, I know a guy who can get you a great seat up front. Join me? Please?" I ask.

Her lip juts out, and she bites it hard, a familiar gesture of indecision. My heart stops for a few moments when it looks like she's going to decline. I'm prepared to launch a persuasive assault when she responds.

"Sure. I'd like that."

I escort Rose to the front of the room where we'll be screening the video. She takes a seat on the aisle, and I pull the 'reserved' sign that's tented on the backrest off before taking my seat next to her.

Across the aisle and a few seats away, Nikki waves at Rose just before Jai hands her a cocktail, caresses her shoulder, then sits beside her. Nikki gives Rose a shy smile, and Rose winks back at her. Fuck, am I really the only person who didn't know about this?

Vince is right, I really am whipped.

"Hey, everyone, thanks for coming. We're about to get started," the hotel events planner announces from a podium beside a large screen. "Everyone, please."

Her request goes unacknowledged, and that's when Vince takes charge. "Hey! Park your ass in a seat. Hurry." His booming voice echoes throughout the room, no microphone needed.

There's a nervous hustle as everyone heads to their seats. When the room settles down, Vince takes a seat next to us.

"Jester's Edge, Wes, Vince, and Jai, all want to thank you for joining them tonight. After the video, they have some announcements to make, some gifts to give out, so please don't dash out to the bar right after."

The lights dim, and Raelynn Tailor's flawless, made-up face fills the entire screen. "Pretty. Little. Liar," she rasps. There's a strobe effect that shifts between Raelynn's face and her journey into the video's dystopian wonderland. By the time's that sequence ends, Raelynn has descended into the dystopian world where Rose and I meet on screen.

It's more than a little arousing to watch this while we sit here together. The scenes are woven together perfectly, and there's no way to tell which sister appears when, except to have lived through the moments together.

I remember as much as see Rose's body arch into mine wearing those leather pants and halter top. It's titillating to sit here, watching, recalling, sharing the secret knowledge of which scenes we've done together and how they made us feel.

As I watch the video, my reaction to Rose is much more potent than it is to Raelynn, even though it's impossible to distinguish between them in the video. I know, and to me, it's obvious. The love scenes with Rose evoke a powerful range of sensations that feel so real, because they were real. Like they are right now.

A painful erection erupts, and I try to control and conceal it by shifting in my chair, alternating my body weight from one hip to another. When I angle my legs toward Rose and cross them, she grips the top of my upper thigh.

Her eyes are shut tight. Little lines of tension have formed at the corners leading to her temples. Her hand scrunches the fabric of my pants, and wrinkles appear as her fingers dig into my thighs.

"Rose," I rasp.

"Oh my God," she answers.

As her fingers squeeze and release my thigh, she evokes a familiar mixture of pleasure and tension that courses through me. All too aware of my surroundings, I place my hand on hers, eager to touch her and cool the heat that blisters between us.

When the video ends and the lights come back on, we're holding hands together like teenagers on a first date. Enthusiastic applause and whistles erupt from the audience. It's a great moment, made even better because we experienced it together.

Vince and Jai make their way up to the podium while they clap and nod thank yous to the audience. When the applause ceases, Jai steps up to the microphone.

"Hey, wow. On behalf of the band, we can't tell you

how much we love this video. Thanks to everyone here who worked too damn hard to make it the reality it is. We've got gift bags for everyone, so make sure to pick those up before you leave. In the meantime, we've also got some special people we want to thank." Jai steps back and Vince takes over.

"I've got to give a special shout out to Darius Lefebre. You're a fucking grandmaster at what you do, and I hope to hell we can do it again." Vince claps in Darius's direction, and the audience joins in.

"Now, I don't this too much, because, well, Jester's Edge is family, and family doesn't spend a lot of time giving each other compliments. But Wes Anders needs to be given extra credit for this video. We all worked hard, but Wes was obsessed with getting it done. And his obsession was the only reason it got done. Wes, buddy… get the hell up here!"

Around me applause starts, and I look over at Rose. She gives my hand a final squeeze before she smiles and claps. Leaving her side is hard, but right now there are things I need to make right.

When I reach the podium, we exchange quick man hugs before I turn back to the audience and enjoy the brief applause before speaking.

"Thank you. We got really lucky with this one. Everyone was so incredible to work with. Darius, Raelynn, so glad to have you both involved in this project." I rub my now sweaty palms together and give a nervous laugh. "But there's one person in particular that deserves as much, if not more credit for getting this done then even I do. Rosalie Tailor."

I point to where she sits and start to clap. Soon, others join. She nods, and smiles at the people around her, then folds her arms in her lap.

"Rosalie not only showed up to the set, on time and in shape to act as a body double for Raelynn Tailor, but she also worked behind the scenes to get all the agents on board, the paperwork done, and the schedules coordinated between everyone, and probably a few metric tons of red tape I don't know about.

"But the thing that impressed me the most, well, maybe the second or third most; the first one I'll keep to myself." There are some oohs and chuckles. "Rosalie is a talented musician, and we were able to collaborate on some fantastic songs. She's working for a well-known composer now, making music for a TV series. We, I, really miss having her around."

There's another round of whistles and cheers, and I look straight at Rosalie's sweet, stunned expression. I smile back and blow her kiss, which elicits a few gasps around the room.

"The second most impressive thing was how hard and fast I fell for her." I gesture to one of the hotel staff waiting in the back, who carries the largest bouquet I've ever seen up to me.

In my time, I've bought one hell of a lot of flowers.

"Come on up here, Sweet Rose. Please let me give these to you."

Tears are rolling down her cheeks, and she covers her mouth while she shakes her head from side-to-side.

"No-o," she mouths to me.

"No?" I repeat.

She shakes her head again.

"Then it looks I'm coming to you."

The bouquet is heavy, and I take special care to ensure the jewelry box hidden deep in the center doesn't fall out as I kneel in front of her and present it to her.

"This is for later." My voice drops to a whisper.

"Later?" she repeats, shocked.

"I want so badly for there to be a later. Give us another chance. Please, Rose?" I pull her fingers inside the bouquet and wrap them around the velvet jewelry box.

"I didn't think you'd ever want me again," she weeps. "I don't believe this."

"Oh God, please believe it. I don't know what I'll do if you don't."

"I believe you. And there's nothing in the world I want more."

Our lips press together in a hard, single, truthful kiss. Around me, I'm aware of chatter and phone cameras, whoops and whistles. All at once it becomes intrusive, and the only place I want to be is alone with Rose.

"Come with me. Now." I don't ask.

CHAPTER FORTY

ROSE

"*T*hank you very much."

From under the covers of the large king-sized bed, I hear Wes speaking to someone at the door of our hotel room. Last night, he rushed me up after the Jester's Edge wrap party, where we did what we do anytime we're alone and there's a horizontal space available.

To say last night was surreal is an understatement.

The first time happened with all the restless fervor that characterizes are our attraction. The second time, though… represented a long satisfying promise of things to come.

Slow and deliberate, like we had all the time in the

world, because neither of us wants to be anywhere or with anyone else.

That promise feels like a dream that I don't want to wake from. I hide under the covers as the sound of a wheeled cart enters the room. Wes inspects the cart and tips the hotel staff. When the door shuts with a thud, I peek out from under the covers in time to see Wes shed the plush hotel robe and sink back on to the bed.

"Rose?" he gives my ass a gentle pat.

"Mmm?" I mumble from under the covers

"You've got to be hungry after last night."

He's right. I sit up and rub my eyes. When I can focus, a beautiful breakfast sits waiting at the foot of the bed. I push the covers away and join him.

"Finally. I've been trying to have breakfast in bed with you for ages."

"This is like a dream." I reach for a perfect, luscious strawberry and dip it in whipped cream.

"Glad you feel that way too."

Wes pours out coffee for both of us, and I suppress an amazed giggle as he makes mine exactly the way I like it.

When did he pick that up?

As he hands me my cup of coffee, his gaze drops to my neck, and he touches the base of my throat with a scowl.

"Damn. We forgot something," he says.

"What?"

"Where are the flowers from last night?"

We spot them at the same time, sitting on the side table near the entrance of the suite. He leaps off the bed, rustles through the blooms, and whistles loudly.

"Here it is," he announces with relief.

My eyes widen at the site of a maroon-red velvet box.

"What is that?" I ask.

He gives me a wolfish smile.

"It's a gift. One intended to impress the hell out of you. Something to make you think sexy, emotional thoughts about me," he says it in a joking way, but I can tell from his expression that this is no joke.

A herd of butterflies flurry inside my stomach as he approaches the bed and sits beside me.

"Open it," he pleads.

I snap the cover open and stare at the contents. "Oh, wow."

It's a necklace. The pendant is two platinum guitars, fused together at their lower bodies and attached to an open-linked, long, platinum chain. Each guitar air hole contains a large colored gem.

"Emerald for me. Blue diamond for you." Wes smooths his finger over one gemstone, then the other.

"Help me put it on." My voice cracks. "Please."

He turns me around, and I pull up my hair while he fastens the safety chain. When he's done, I stand up, grasp his hand, and pull him toward the nearest mirror.

"It's amazing. Thank you."

The v-shape of the guitars frame the base of my throat, a precious gem on either side. When I swallow, the guitars move against the skin of my neck, as the gems catch the ambient glow from the overhead lights.

"I wanted to give you something you'd like. Something that would let you know I was serious but not in a rush. We can go as fast or slow as you want."

I steady his sweet, intense expression in the mirror before slumping back against his chest and heaving a sigh of relief.

"Music to my ears," I tell him.

"Really?" His tone is pensive and calm.

"We've done fast. Love it. But… I don't want us to crash and burn, because you mean so much to me."

He says nothing, simply bends close to my ear and nuzzles my neck.

"I feel like I know you in deep, intimate ways." I swallow hard and the gems at my throat catch the light again. "But when I ask myself what your favorite color or restaurant is, or how you feel when I borrow your favorite sweatshirt… I don't know. But I want to."

"Let me get this straight," he brushes his lips against my temple. "You want to go out on dates?"

"Yes," I reply with enthusiasm.

"Have sleepovers?" he asks.

"At both of our houses."

"Take vacations together?"

"To destinations we both agree on and can afford."

"Separate careers?"

Completely." I'm firm. "At least for now."

Wes moans, then plants a soft kiss on my mouth. Then he looks me straight in the eye.

"It sounds like you want a boyfriend, as opposed to a sugar daddy or a fuck buddy," he says.

"That's exactly what I want. For now." My gaze meets his.

He nods, the faintest hint of a smile curling at the side

of his mouth. "You, know. I'm good with that, too. For now."

EPILOGUE

ROSE AND WES

"*T*he Award for Music Composition for a
Limited Series or Movie goes to… Rose Tailor
Anders!"

My body remains frozen, and my head explodes as it
tries to comprehend what's happened. It's late now, the
bigger categories announced what seems like ages ago.
But around me the applause still rings out with enthusiasm, along with familiar music and a large screen on stage
that displays images of the show whose music I
composed.

"That's you, babe," Wes whispers before planting a
huge kiss on my lips, then touching up the corner of my
lipstick with his thumb like he's done countless times
before. "You DID it! YOU did it!"

"This must be a mistake," I reply.

I search Wes's eyes for confirmation. What I see there takes what little breath is left in me away.

His expression is a mix of awe, tenderness, and pride. From the amazement in his voice to the tears in his eyes, it's a moment I'll never forget, award be damned.

"No mistake," he promises me. "Looks like Zombie Dystopia really is your thing after all."

"Who knew all I needed was a mutant time-traveling heroine immune to zombieism and an evolved Zombie King sharing in the hard work of making babies uniquely adapted to an uncertain future to inspire my creativity?" I give a nervous laugh.

"When it clicks, it clicks." Wes stands and offers me his hand. He knows there's no way for me and this huge baby belly to get out of this tiny chair without help.

"Thank you." I tell him. "For clicking with me."

He pulls me up, exerting considerable strength while making it look effortless. That sums up our entire relationship. The man is a rock. A driven, creative force that revels in pushing the envelope, exploring new boundaries, and enabling the people he loves around him.

Wes drags his hands over the top of my baby bump and rests them on either side of my non-existent waist as he gives me a protective nudge toward the aisle. He aims us toward the stage and walks alongside me, one hand on the small of my back, while the other cups my elbow.

When you're seven months pregnant with twins, you don't hurry anywhere. Seriously, top speed is a waddle right now. Watching us approach the stage on the large overhead screen, I'm grateful for the exhaustion that prevented an argument with Raelynn when she insisted on styling me for this event. I don't know how she managed it, but this deep India orange gown with the full skirts make my boys look more like oversized beachballs instead of a pair of hippity hops.

Yeah, they're boys.

Twins run in the Tailor family, and I have a strong suspicion that our sons are identical twins, just like me and Raelynn. When we're home, leading our most creative, quiet lives, I can picture two boys with Wes's killer looks and charm, and if they possess half his talent between them, lord help the ladies of their generation.

It's been almost four years since that song we wrote in his basement between endless days and sex-filled sleepless nights found its way to the top of the charts. For Wes, it was another day at the office, but for me it was a life-altering occurrence.

Overnight, my professional prospects changed. Music producers were suddenly returning my calls. Hell, some even called me out of the blue, just like Carl Christensen told me would happen. But I stuck with my job, because I learned almost as much from Carl as I did from Wes, musically speaking. It also offered a steady paycheck, which came in handy when life pitched its next curveball.

In another twist, I lived with Nikki and Rachel for a year. They knew someone from their school who was going abroad for a year who rented them a three-bedroom house closer to where they worked. They offered me the third spot, and I accepted. Wes and I weren't ready to move in together, and I hadn't lived independently since I first moved to the city.

It ended up being one of the best years of my life. Living with friends did wonders for my self-confidence, and it gave Wes and I a courtship period that we'd never had.

We fell even more in love. We wrote beautiful music together. Seriously. Beautiful music.

My work with Carl ended a year later, as predicted. After that, I worked for the band again, but things were never open ended. I always had another gig lined up and ready to start, which was super important to both of us. I never wanted to be dependent on Wes for my career, and he respected that.

I'm forever grateful to him.

As I approach the stairs to the podium, two ushers wearing tuxedos each extend an arm to me.

"You got this, girl. Now go and get it," Wes says, handing me over to them.

All of this is raging through my mind when I find myself being congratulated by a once famous pop star turned top tier music director and an iconic voice actor.

"Wow, this is amazing. Thank you," I start slowly. "It's hard to know what to say, because, come on, we all thought this award was going to *Whispers from Heaven*. Well, I did anyway." I clear my throat.

"If you'd told me when my grandparents bought me my first guitar or when I went off to study music that I'd be standing on this stage right now, accepting this award, I probably would've rolled my eyes and wrote a song about a particularly bizarre and amazing dream.

"It sounds cliché, but there really are so many people I need to thank for this. My best friend Nicole, who convinced me that moving here would be a great decision. Carl Christensen who taught me so much. The session musicians who always, always show up and give one hundred and ten percent.

And then there's Wes." My voice cracks with emotion. "My everything. Who found me when I was hiding, believed in me when I didn't, and was generous with his unconditional support and love; I would not be here without him. Truth. Thank you."

As I step away from the podium and look down at the gilded three-pound goddess in my hand, the ushers return, each one taking me by an elbow and leading me away.

Enough.

The vibe backstage after the ceremony is informal and energetic. But Rosalie has been running on adrenaline for the past few days, and she looks like she's ready to collapse. From across the room where I've just procured a few cold bottled waters, her dark under eye shadows stand out, and her hips jut forward the way they do when her back is killing her.

"Drink this," I insist, inserting myself into the group. My arm slips around her back and she leans in gratefully.

"Hon, I can't drink any more tonight."

That's it.

I flash my best smile to her friends, old and new, mostly other winners of musical categories. "It's been one hell of an evening, but I think it's time to get my very pregnant wife home. What do you say, Rose?"

She heaves a relived sigh. "I'd love to stay here all night and talk with you, but my boys are kicking like soccer players."

"You'll just have to be nominated again when you're not seven and a half months pregnant," Marcus, one of the studio musicians, tells her.

"Right. By that time, I'll be worried about my walker fitting through the door."

"Don't sell yourself short," he scolds.

"Thank you," I reply. Maybe if Rose hears it from others, she'll listen.

"They're both boys?" Stella, another composer holding a statue, asks."

"Yes, and I can't wait to meet them," Rose answers.

"Go home and rest," Stella insists. "We're all around, and we can see each other in few days."

We say our goodbyes, and Rose melts into my side underneath my arm as we head for the exit.

"Rose, I'm sorry but you looked ready to collapse," I tell her at the curb while we wait for our driver.

"You weren't wrong. Thanks for doing what you did."

My response is a kiss on her temple, while my knuckles press into familiar, intimate spots on her lower back. She rewards me with a purr that sends a rush of blood straight to my groin.

Damn. Five years later and she can still do this to me. I'm a fucking lucky man.

"Wes," her voice rasps at my throat. "Are you working tomorrow?"

"Always. But… I don't have to be anywhere and no one's coming over. Why?"

"Well, this has all been like a fairytale. But... there's one more thing that would make it complete."

"What's that?"

Rose loops her fingers between my belt buckle and pants. "I could sure use some celebratory sex. "Are you up for it?"

"Always. But how about you?" I stroke her shoulder and turn her toward me so she can feel me up with as much privacy as we can hope for outside by the curb.

Where the hell is the limo?

"I need a hot bath, a little rest, and maybe a backrub. But these pregnancy hormones make me horny twenty-four seven, plus the orgasms are out of this world. I want to enjoy everything while it lasts."

"Your wish is my command," I whisper before my lips brush hers.

"Rock star."

"Don't ever forget it."

THANK YOU FOR READING!

Reviews help authors keep writing. Thank you!

Please consider leaving a review *on Bookbub or your favorite booksellers*

website. Reviews help authors keep writing. Thank you!

ALSO BY ANNABETH SARYU

The Hearts So Fine Series

Fighting Hearts

Crazy Hearts

Tender Hearts

CASINO PLAYERS SAGA

Please note, this is a serial and all the episodes are intended to be read in the following order:

BOXED SET

Book One, All In, *digital format only*

Book Two, Double or Nothing, *digital format only*

Book Three, Ante Up, *digital format only*

STANDALONES:

Wish Up On a Rockstar

ABOUT THE AUTHOR

Annabeth writes steamy contemporary romances that explore the edges of passion and possibility. Her stories contain characters who exude emotional awareness and authentic human weakness as they journey towards their happily ever afters.

Away from the keyboard, she loves to travel, read and bike, in addition to helping with school activities. She calls creative-friendly Austin, TX home, where her family and menagerie of pets keep her company while she's at the keyboard.

You can find her at her website, https://annabethsaryu.com

BB bookbub.com/profile/annabeth-saryu

f facebook.com/authorannabethsaryu

a amazon.com/author/annabethsaryu

instagram.com/annabethsaryu

www.ingramcontent.com/pod-product-compliance
Lightning Source LLC
Chambersburg PA
CBHW052026240626
47153CB00006B/1969